Summer in Manhattan

KATHERINE GARBERA

A division of HarperCollins*Publishers*
www.harpercollins.co.uk

Harper*Impulse* an imprint of
HarperCollins*Publishers*
The News Building
1 London Bridge Street
London SE1 9GF

www.harpercollins.co.uk

This paperback edition 2017

First published in Great Britain in ebook format by HarperCollins*Publishers* 2017

A catalogue record for this book
is available from the British Library

ISBN: 9780008142544

Typeset in Minion by Palimpsest Book Production Ltd, Falkirk, Stirlingshire

Printed and bound in Great Britain

At this heart of this book are friendships and the bonds of family and motherhood, so it's dedicated to the women who have been my role models and soul sisters. They are Charlotte Smith, Rose Wilkenson, Priscilla Tromblay, Linda Harris, Donna Scammerhorn, Mimi Wells, Eve Gaddy, Nancy Robards Thompson and Barbara Padlo. At different times in my life I have looked to you all for strength and support and never been let down.

Chapter 1

Sunny, summery, perfect.

That was all Cici Johnson thought as she walked out the front door of her building on New York's Upper East Side. She'd been living in the City for more than five years. She'd gone into business with her two best friends, Hayley and Iona, and they were the toast of the town thanks to Valentine's Day and their new chocolate making classes. But like Hayley said, give a girl chocolate and she's happy for one day; teach a girl to make her own and she'll be happy forever.

Or something like that.

But then Hayley was in the flush of new love so everything seemed so great and optimistic for her. She wasn't on skid row with her relationship, which was the way Cici seemed to be.

Numbers were her game and always had been. For most of her life, she didn't realize that everyone didn't see numbers in their head the way that she did. In fact, she'd rather deal with a spreadsheet or analyze statistics any day than have to try to figure out people.

Bad ass number cruncher, she thought, as she pulled her horn-rimmed glasses from her bag and put them on. As if being a math nerd wasn't enough, she was also pretty much blind without her glasses on.

"Looking good, Cici," Hayley said with a wave as Cici approached Sant Ambroeus, an upscale Italian espresso bar and restaurant. When they'd been in the planning stages of the Candied Apple & Café they'd spent a lot of time here drinking espresso and eating cornetti, a fancy word for Italian croissants. These days, Cici was cutting back on her caffeine intake but she had found she loved the smell of it and her friends were indulging.

"Hey, girl. I guess that week in Jamaica didn't kill you," Cici said with a laugh.

"Not in the least. And you and Io didn't have any problems at the Candied Apple & Café," Hayley replied, pulling her close for a hug. Her friend looked tanned and completely relaxed. As much as she hated to admit it, it seemed like finding a guy and falling in love had been good for Hayley.

Hayley had cut her hair on her last birthday and decided it was time to be someone new. To stop trying to please everyone and just do what felt right to her. And it had worked. Cici wondered if *she* could do that too. Cut her hair and change her life?

"Where's Io?"

"Running late," Cici said. "I think she's still trying to get a decent rent for the new place she wants to open near Town Hall."

"She's such a property diva. She should have her own show," Hayley said as they went inside and were seated.

"Cappuccino," Hayley said.

"Green tea," Cici asked for as she eyed the espresso machine in the back longingly.

Their waiter, Alfonso, put his hand on Cici's shoulder. "Stay strong bella."

"Ha," Cici said, sitting back in her chair. She put her hand on her stomach. She was ten weeks pregnant. Not a big deal. But she'd been hiding it from her friends and family since she'd … well, she'd done something dumb.

Well, it was only dumb when you factored in that she'd slept with one man to get back at another. A man she liked, in fact. A man who was very much in her life all the time, since he was the best friend of Hayley's fiancé. Yeah, it was as awkward as you might have guessed.

"Before Io gets here …"

"What? Is something wrong?"

"No not at all. I was hoping you'd come and stay at my place while you're pregnant. I know your folks are travelling this summer and I wanted you to have someone close. Plus, Garrett wants me to move into his place. And Dad will rent mine out."

"I don't know," Cici replied. She was already in the process of moving closer to the city. She'd sublet her place in Queens and had her eye on a very ritzy Upper East Side apartment.

"The rent would be really low. It's price-fixed since Dad owns the place and he paid it off before my mom died."

If she moved into Hayley's brownstone, she'd have a greater chance of running into Hoop and she'd done a good job of avoiding him for the last few weeks. Did she really want to ruin that?

"I'll think about it. I already signed a contract to move into an apartment not too far from here. I bet Io would love to take your place. Her mom is always trying to set her up with a nice Greek guy."

"My mom is unstoppable," Iona remarked as she sat down at their table. "Sorry I'm late. What were you talking about? Besides my nightmare."

"You have a Mom who loves you and only wants what is best for you," Hayley said with a cheeky grin. "That's not a nightmare."

She'd have liked the close relationship that Iona had with her mom, Cici thought.

"Yeah, well, you're not the one who's supposed to go to the Hamptons in two weeks to meet some family friends. Uh, I know all of our family friends and so who could she possible have dragged into the mix?" Iona asked. "I'll tell you who … some

3

single guy from a *good* Greek family. I know she's been to see the matchmaker."

The waiter came back with their drinks and Iona ordered a double espresso before he left.

"Maybe the matchmaker will be the right thing for you," Cici said. "I mean, if I learned anything watching reality TV ..."

"It's that your best-friend is going to torture you with the smell of coffee all day if you don't stop trying to convince her that being set up by a matchmaker is a good idea?" Iona quipped.

Cici laughed and shook her head, holding her hands up at her shoulders. "Fine. I'll stop."

"That's better. So, what were you talking about?" Iona asked as she lined up her sugar substitute packets for her espresso.

"Hayley wants me to move into her place but I just signed a lease on an apartment so I can't," Cici said. Thank heavens she'd signed that lease yesterday. It was the only way she was getting out of this. She knew her friends cared about her. But they were different than she was. They seemed to waltz through life making the right choices ... heck, even their bad choices turned out okay.

"Wow, dodged that bullet," Iona said.

Cici kicked her friend under the table.

"What are you talking about?" Hayley asked after taking a sip of her cappuccino.

"She's trying to avoid Garrett's friend Hoop."

"You are?" Hayley asked, blushing as she did so.

"Yes."

"Why?" Hayley leaned in, her blonde hair swinging forward against the side of her face.

Cici looked down at her lap, her own bangs falling over her glasses and she tried to find a way to say this next part without sounding like a woman who'd done something she regretted. She decided when she'd discovered her pregnancy that she'd try to embrace it. Even though she had always assumed she'd never have a kid of her own. Cici relished the idea of herself as the cool Auntie.

"I just don't think it's wise to get involved with someone who's friends with Garrett," she said. Actually, Hoop had said it first all three months ago when they'd been at Olympus and had shared one hot kiss.

Not hot enough for him? Too hot for him? She didn't know. All she knew was that he'd seen her to a cab and sent her home alone.

"Is this because of …" Hayley gestured to Cici's stomach.

"My pregnancy? Yes, that's part of it," Cici said. "Let's talk about something else. Something fun for the summer at the Candied Apple & Café."

Cici turned the conversation to business and was happy enough when they finished breakfast and she waved her friends goodbye. She was on a week's vacation from the Candied Apple & Café so didn't have to be in the office. It was a forced vacation of sorts, since Hayley had been on one and Iona was going to be spending a week in the Hamptons. Her friends had insisted she take a break as well.

She'd decided to move into her new apartment and try adjusting to being pregnant. Cici knew her life was about to change forever.

Jason Hooper, known to everyone as Hoop, had screwed up. It wasn't the first time. After all, he was thirty-three and had been a cop for five years before giving it up to become an attorney. Growing up in the foster system had honed his natural instincts of being a loner. He let people in but it took him a while to decide if he should let them stay. He wanted to say that was where he'd made his mistake with Cici. He'd needed time to think. To plug the facts into a pro/con list and then decide if the heat between the two of them was worth exploring.

Stupid.

Now, he was drinking club soda but it tasted like regret as he watched her talking with her friends and mingling in a way that kept her far away from him as she worked the room at the summer kickoff party at the Candied Apple & Café.

Manhattan's trendiest new chocolate shop was on a roll and if the crowd at tonight's event was anything to go by, they were going to continue that momentum for a long time.

Cici Johnson, with her short wavy hair, thick rimmed glasses and curvy figure was temptation incarnate. But his track record with the opposite sex wasn't the best. He didn't do long term and it had seemed wise to him to avoid any kind of complications that would impact his friendship with Garrett.

Idiot.

"Dude, you're staring at her," Garrett Mulligan observed, handing him a beer.

Hoop dumped his club soda on the tray of a passing waiter and took the beer from Garrett. Garrett was his best friend and a cop. They'd known each other since high school when Garrett's parents had become his surrogate family. Garrett was the reason why he'd screwed up with Cici.

"It's all your fault."

"How do you figure?" Garrett asked.

"If you hadn't been dating Hayley then I could have comfortably had my usual fling with Cici and moved on."

"If I hadn't been dating Hayley you never would have met her."

"Fair point."

Hoop took a swallow of his beer and skimmed the room, hoping that some other woman would catch his eye. But no one did. It was Cici for him. It was as if the moment he'd told her that a few hot kisses were all they'd ever share, fate had a deep chuckle at his expense and made her impossible to forget.

"So …"

"So?"

"Are you going to go talk to her or continue to try to stare her down from here?" Garrett asked.

The party was to celebrate the start of summer and a new menu at the Candied Apple & Café. The trendy Fifth Avenue confectionery that was co-owned by Garrett's fiancée Hayley, Cici and their friend Iona.

"Possibly. She's been avoiding me. I've called her a dozen times."

"I've never known you to let something like that stop you," Garrett remarked with a laugh.

Hoop thought about it, and then finished his beer with one deep swallow. He wasn't going to let it stop him. He couldn't. He had been dating a lot the last three months since their one date. Sad that he knew exactly how long it had been, but there it was. Every time he leaned in to kiss another woman, he compared it to Cici. Every time he made another woman laugh, he remembered how much he liked Cici's laugh. Maybe it was that he'd put her off limits. Something that could be easily fixed if he could go out on one date with her. But she had moved on.

Now he was panting after her … well not exactly panting … but close enough.

He handed his empty bottle to a passing waiter and moved through the throng of party goers toward Cici. She wore a sundress that hugged her endless curves and ended just above her knees. It was a straight sort of A-line skirt with a fitted bodice and as he got closer he noticed that she wore a thin gold necklace and the charm had moved around to nestle at the back of her neck.

She said something he couldn't hear and the man she was talking to responded and then she laughed. He felt a bolt of awareness go through him along with a tinge of jealousy. Another man had made her laugh.

He knew it was irrational. He'd been the one to push her away, but this weird emotion that she inspired in him wasn't rational.

"Cici," he said softly, coming up behind her and putting his hand on the small of her back. "It's been too long since I've seen you."

She tensed immediately and he noticed that goose pimples

spread down her arm as she turned to look at him. She pushed her glasses up her nose. Her bow-shaped mouth parted and her lips seemed to beckon him, but he knew that was just his own desires and not necessarily hers.

"Hoop. I didn't realize you were at the party," she said. "Do you know Theo? He's Iona's brother."

"I do," Hoop said, holding his hand out toward the young Greek man. Iona's brother looked like he should be in Hollywood, starring in the big movies. Not tending bar three nights a week at a night club and DJing in his spare time. Theo shook his hand and then moved on to talk to another group of people.

Cici delicately took a step to the left, breaking contact with the hand he'd placed on her back.

"How have you been?" she asked.

"Not bad. How about yourself?" he countered. Small talk. Really? This was what he was reduced to.

"I'm okay. Listen, I'm really embarrassed that I haven't called you back," she said.

"You are?"

"Yes. It's awkward, right? Our best friends are engaged and I'm dodging your calls. It's just, I was embarrassed after that night we all went out."

Hoop was afraid it was something like that. He had been so firm in saying no to her. "Well, I'm the one who screwed up and I'd appreciate it if you'd let me make it up to you."

"How?" she asked.

"Drinks. Nothing too heavy, just drinks."

How about lame, how much lamer could this get? But the fact that he hadn't been able to forget her had knocked him off balance. Made him wonder what it was his conscious mind didn't see that his subconscious did.

"I can't. I'm … I just can't," she said quickly, walking away without a backward glance.

He stood there.

Fair enough, he thought, but another part of him didn't want to let her go.

He followed her out onto the terrace that overlooked Central Park. The sun was setting and she stood near the edge of the balcony with her face turned toward the tepid breeze that blew.

"Why?" he asked, staying where he was just on the threshold of the balcony.

"Why what?" she too asked, turning toward him. The wind blew her curly hair around her face and she reached up to push a strand back behind her ear.

"I guess I should have said why not?" he elaborated.

"Our friends are engaged now. They were just dating before," she said. "Nothing has really changed. And I don't want to have to start avoiding them."

"What if things worked out between us?" he asked, taking a step closer.

"If you really believed that you wouldn't have pushed me away that night at Olympus," she said. "Let's just be friends."

"Friends?"

"We can do that right?"

"Yes," he said. But inside, every male instinct he had said no. He'd been friend-zoned by the one woman who he couldn't get out of his head. She haunted him night and day. He saw her in his dreams and thought of her when a meeting at work droned on. So how was he going to be "just friends" with her now?

Cici spent the next week avoiding her friends and staying in her office. She had to file their quarterly earnings so she was kept busy. She kept the door to her office closed but she still could hear the bustle of Hayley and her staff working in the kitchen.

Carolyn, the assistant manager of the store, had been bringing her fresh strawberries dipped in chocolate and apple and seltzer water iced drinks that kept Cici cool while she worked.

"Figured you could use one of these," Carolyn said.

The other woman was five foot, five inches tall and wore her brown hair in a high ponytail. She had an easy smile and an aggressive eye for retail space. Every time Carolyn came into her office Cici suspected the woman was going to ask for more money.

"Thanks, I am thirsty."

"Good, got a minute?" Carolyn asked.

"I do, but your budget is fixed," Cici said with a smile as she took a sip of her cool drink.

"Oh, it's not about the store. I heard you were subletting your place in Queens …"

"I am. But I already found someone," Cici replied. "I didn't know you were looking for a place."

"I'm not really. Just thought I'd see what the rent was. My place is smallish."

"I'll keep my ear out," Cici said.

"Thanks," Carolyn said. "I'll let you get back to it. Do you want your door closed?"

"Yes please. I need quiet for my work."

But it was a lie. She was hiding.

She knew it and she suspected her friends did too, but they were giving her space.

She was the first of their group to be pregnant and she suspected, just like her, they didn't know what to expect. Her mom, who Cici still hadn't told about the pregnancy, had been texting her every day.

For some reason her mom had never fully grasped that her adult daughter had a real job and bills. She still wanted Cici to go on every family vacation and be available for any family gathering at the drop of a hat.

That's why when her phone buzzed she ignored it. She didn't want to see another smiling photo of her mom, stepdad and twin half-brothers on the steps of Machu Picchu.

She finished tallying up the last column of numbers and then set it aside to take another sip of her drink.

She picked up the phone, surprised that the message was from Hoop and not her parents.

Hoop: *Hello, it's Hoop. Hayley gave me your number. I've got an extra ticket to the Yankees game on Friday. Heard you're a baseball fan. Wanna go? Just friends! :)*

She leaned back in her chair and looked at the ceiling in her office. It was a faux exposed beam and plaster number that made the building seem like an idealized French country farmhouse.

Baseball. She loved the game. Before the twins were born, she and her stepdad had gone to every game. Her love of numbers had served her well because she remembered all the stats of players. She might not be able to remember other things but those stats had stayed with her.

Cici: *Okay.*

Hoop: *Great. What's your address? I'll pick you up.*

Cici: *I can meet you there.*

Hoop: *Friends, right?*

She sighed. This friend thing wasn't as easy as she hoped. She was walking a fine line between letting him into her life and keeping him at arm's length.

Cici: *Yeah. Here's my address.*

Hoop: *See you on Friday.*

Cici: *See ya.*

She stood up and walked out of her office, determined to politely tell Hayley to stop playing go between with her and Hoop. But her friend was busy with one of the new apprentice candy makers at the marble countertops. So Cici walked into the retail shop instead.

They were busy for mid-afternoon but it was late May and some tourists whose kids were already out of school were taking a break from the heat and enjoying their famous Candied Apple & Café milkshakes.

She waved at the manager as she walked through the store and

11

out onto the street. Immediately she wished she'd brought her sunglasses but she didn't want to go back inside. Not yet.

She felt restless and she admitted to herself as she walked up Fifth Avenue, past all the shops and tourists, a little bit scared. When she got to St Patrick's Cathedral, Cici walked up the steps and into the church.

It was cool and quiet inside and she made her way to one of the pews in the back of the church. She took a seat on the cold wooden bench and closed her eyes. In her head were images of the church from when she was younger and she heard the hymns of her youth playing in her mind. She sat there and quietly prayed as she did most days.

For guidance.

She had spent most of her life managing one crisis or another brought on by her impulsive behavior and she knew that she had to change. She wanted to give her child the best in life, starting with a good parent.

She didn't think about the man she'd slept with or the fact that when she'd called him he'd said he wanted nothing to do with her or the baby.

That was in the past. She'd find a way to bring her baby up and shower him or her with so much love they'd always feel wanted.

That was all she could do.

She put the kneeler down and then said the prayers she'd learned growing up. Just the familiar words, soothing her troubled soul, and bringing her a surcease from her thoughts.

When she was done, she put some folded bills from her pocket in the collection box and went back outside.

She was going to have to figure out how to be friends with Hoop. Actual *friends*. Because every time she saw his name she felt a little thrill go through her and she knew that wasn't a good idea.

In fact, going to a baseball game with him wasn't smart either.

Before she could change her mind, she pulled out her phone and texted him she couldn't make it.

She didn't need another complication in her life right now and it felt like Hoop could be a very big one. She went back to work, filed the taxes and then spent the rest of the day in her new apartment.

She was avoiding Hayley, who'd tried talking to her about Hoop, and Iona, who wanted to go shopping for baby clothes with her. Cici realized that before anything else, she really needed to find her own inner strength.

Chapter 2

Cici's apartment was slowly coming together. It was different from the house in Queens and she hoped that it represented her new life with her baby. She put her hand over her stomach, as was becoming a habit, as if by touch she would be able to connect to the child who was still more of a hazy idea than reality to her.

She sat down on the two-seater couch with overstuffed cushions, leaning on the patterned throw pillow. She put her feet up on the glass coffee table and looked around the apartment.

She'd worked hard for this place and felt a real sense of pride that she'd earned this. The sweeping curved staircase led to the upper floor and her bedroom and the room she was going to make into the nursery. It was a pre-war apartment building that had been completely redone. Her living room had a fireplace with built in bookcases on either side and she'd lined the shelves with her favorite books. Her childhood favorites by authors like E.L. Konigsburg, Madeleine L'Engle and her collection of Trixie Belden books. She'd started a collection of Dr. Seuss books for the baby. The next shelves held her paperback collection of romance novels, thrillers and of course all the Harry Potter books.

She had pictures on the shelf as well. One of her, Hayley and Iona on the day they'd opened the Candied Apple & Café. Even seated across the room she could still see those big grins on their faces. The sense of joy and happiness she got from her job and her friendship with those women … well, that was something she hoped she could give her child too.

Her child.

Sometimes it still didn't seem real.

She had tried to reach out to Rich … the man who'd fathered her child, but he really didn't want to be part of her life or the baby's. She got it. She was the one who was carrying the kid and even she was dealing with, well, the unreality of it. And as Rich had pointed out, they barely knew each other. It had been a wedding party hook up. Not forever.

She let her head fall back on the edge of the couch and looked up at the ceiling with its ornate trim and realized that no matter how together this apartment looked, she was still a complete mess on the inside.

The timer on her smart phone went off and she jumped up. She had plans tonight. Shakespeare in the park. One of her favorite things about summer.

She got changed into a flowy summery top and a pair of white jeans that were actually a little loose on her thanks to all the morning sickness, and then she opted to skip putting in her contacts and grabbed her prescription sunglasses instead.

She took a look at herself in the mirror, her curly hair was actually not too frizzy tonight and she turned sideways to check herself out. Then she put her hands under the flowy top and pushed it out a little bit. That's what she was going to look like soon. When the baby started showing.

She pulled her hands out and smoothed the top back into place.

"I don't regret you, bean," she whispered, and then filled her mind with love for the unborn child that resided there. Ten weeks pregnant. And definitely on her own with the baby.

No regrets.

*

She left her apartment and walked through Central Park to her seat. She was ready to relax, sip her juice smoothie and let Beatrice and Benedict sweep her away. She was going to forget that she was almost three months pregnant and alone.

"Excuse me."

She glanced up to see a latecomer making his way down the row behind her. She really had no tolerance for people who came to shows late. It wasn't like they hadn't printed the time on the ticket. But then she was chronically early for everything. She glanced at the seat next to her that was still empty.

Let it stay empty.

She noticed the man on her left standing and realized that the person holding the ticket for the seat next to hers was finally here.

She stood up to let him go by, glancing up with a smile on her face that froze as she looked into those familiar sky blue eyes.

"Hoop."

"Cici," he said. "Funny running into you here."

Yeah, funny.

She sat down after he went past her, pulling her phone out of her bag. How could Hayley set her up like this?

"Don't blame Hayley," Hoop said. "I made her do it."

"Why?" Cici replied.

"It just felt like we needed to clear the air," he said. "And I hesitated with you before and screwed up so this time … I'm not going to do that again. I'll tell you all about it after the play. I made us dinner reservations at a nearby restaurant."

"I'm not sure that's a good idea," Cici said, her stomach sinking. She couldn't start a new relationship right now. She wasn't in the right frame of mind and she wasn't even sure what her life was going to be in six months' time when she gave birth to the baby.

"Please, Cici, give me a chance to make up for the way I behaved that night. The truth is we had a real connection and that scared me," he said.

She didn't want to hear him saying things she had wished he'd said that first night. She glanced down at the round stage set up at the bottom of the bleachers and then further on to the castle with the flag flying. She wanted to believe that this was a true second chance.

If she hadn't been so emotional and determined to prove that she was still attractive to other men that night in February this wouldn't be an issue. But she'd always let her temper get the better of her.

And no matter what Hoop thought at this moment, she knew that no man wanted to raise another man's child. She knew it first-hand. Her stepfather was nice but he wasn't a dad to her. Not the way he was to his own kids, her half siblings, and she wanted more for her baby. And for herself.

"I ... things have changed Hoop."

"How?" he asked.

She glanced again at the stage, willing Don Pedro to come out on stage and start the show, but they still had a good five minutes before that would happen.

She took a deep breath and that didn't help. She took a sip of her smoothie. Hoop reached over and put his hand on hers.

"What is it you are trying to tell me?" he asked.

"I'm pregnant."

There. She'd said it.

"What?" he asked, sitting back in his seat, trying to process what he'd just heard.

"I'm having a baby," she said.

"And the dad? Oh, God, is that why you have been avoiding me?" he asked. "I shouldn't have pushed the way I did. You said friends and I'm here like, 'let's start over.'"

She put her hand on his arm.

"The dad is out of the picture. It's embarrassing, Hoop. And honestly, I don't want to talk about it."

"Fair enough," he said.

She stared at him in the deepening twilight. He had a classically beautiful face, strong masculine jaw, high cheekbones and there was some emotion in his eyes that she couldn't read.

He'd made a decision at the Olympus nightclub when they'd met, one that had set her on this course and she knew there was no way to change it. In fact, she wouldn't change it. *She wouldn't change it.* She and the bean were going to be a team and they'd have each other's back. Not like her mom when she'd married her stepdad and started a new family with him…

Or at least that was the plan. So far, it was nothing more than a new attitude and some determination, but she'd always been able to make things happen and she knew that this would be no different.

Pregnant.

He didn't know how to react to that. It was the last thing he'd expected. He understood now why she'd been so hesitant to see him again. And he'd said they'd be friends … he could do that, right?

He had no idea.

A kid.

Children.

They were complicated.

He avoided them whenever possible. Knew how fragile life was for a child. Families fell apart, kids ended up in the system and if they were like him they ended up in a lot of homes before they found a real one.

He did his part working with the Big Brothers Big Sisters organization but dating a woman who was pregnant … well, she didn't want to date so that wasn't an issue.

Frankly, his mind was slammed with a bunch of different scenarios on how to deal with this and the one that would be the easiest would be to be friendly until the end of the first act, fake an emergency work text and leave. Except he was a man and his foster father, the one he thought of as his dad, had raised him to take the right path; not the easy one.

Hoop had grown up in foster care until he'd finally made it to the Fillions'. The man had been gruff and to be honest it had been more of a halfway house where Hoop had been faced with shaping up or going to jail. Pops had reached him somehow and set him on the path he was on now.

"Want to bolt, don't you?" she asked. She didn't take her eyes off the stage but he knew all of her concentration was on him.

"Yeah. But I won't."

"Why not?" she asked, turning to face him. Those blue eyes of hers behind her dark rimmed glasses were guarded and she had a bead of sweat on her upper lip.

He reached over and brushed it off with his thumb and felt that zing go through him. There was a connection between the two of them and if he hadn't tried to ignore it when they'd first met, well, maybe things would be different. But they weren't.

"I can't get you out of my head, Cici," he admitted. "And running from you, from this ..." he gestured to the two of them, "didn't really help me before."

"I'm not the same woman you first met," she said.

"Of course not. But I'd still like to get to know you better," he said.

She sighed.

That didn't bode well for his chances of even having dinner with her tonight.

"That's a no, isn't it?"

"Yes. It's not you, it's me. I mean, *really* me."

"Pipe down over there, the show is starting."

Cici flushed and then turned to face the stage as Don Pedro came on and *Much Ado About Nothing* started. Hoop wanted to take her hand and lead her away from here but he noticed that Cici sank back into her seat, took a sip of her smoothie and was entranced by the play. She watched it carefully, laughing at times, and even though this was one of Hoop's favorite Shakespeare plays, he watched her instead of the action.

When the production was over and they filed out of their seats, he knew she was ready to leave.

"I have that dinner reservation," he said.

"I know. I'm hungry."

"Then come and eat with me. We can talk and get to know each other better. No pressure or anything. Just a guy and a girl."

"But we're not just a guy and a girl."

He took her hand in his and started walking on the path that lead to Central Park West and the restaurant he'd booked. "Tonight we are. Just for tonight. We never had a real date."

"No we didn't," she said. "I really liked you."

"I know. I think it freaked me out a little," he admitted. He wished it hadn't but he knew that he liked things, relationships, to be light and uncomplicated and Cici had felt even then like she'd demand more.

"And it's not freaking you out now?"

"Nope," he said. "Not tonight. I think you need a night out and I could use one too."

"Okay but this is just one night. That's it. Dinner and then I get a cab home."

"Dinner and then we can see what happens."

She nibbled her lower lip and narrowed her eyes at him. "What do you want to happen?"

"I have no idea, Cici. You are always throwing my carefully made plans into chaos, so I never know what to expect."

"Just dinner. That's it."

He nodded, but he knew he wanted more. Even as he was making small talk about the play, he was very aware that Cici was different. And one dinner date was never going to satisfy him.

But she wasn't in a place for anything more. And Hoop would respect that. He would be the friend he knew she'd need. He worked with foster kids and with their birth mothers' pro bono, trying to bring together families that were broken. He knew how complicated it could be and wanted more than that for Cici.

"Why are you watching me?"

"Just trying to remind myself that you need a friend and not a lover," he said.

She tipped her head to the side, studying him. "Let's start with the friend and then we'll see about the other."

"Well, friend, why do you love Shakespeare?" he asked.

"Why do you?" she countered.

"When I was growing up, someone gave me a copy of *The Tempest*. It was addictive. I loved the story and it gave me something to do at night. I was a bit of a troublemaker for a while and had a curfew so if I broke it … I'd go to jail."

"You were a bad boy?"

"Yes, but not as bad as I could have been. And that's not as glamorous as it might seem."

"I was a good girl. If there was a rule, I followed it. Actually, if I even thought something might be a rule I didn't break it."

"I can see that," he said. "But you've got a wild side too."

"Don't we all," she said smiling.

"I'm not sure about that. I really don't anymore," he said.

"Well, I'm not sure I'm all that wild. It's just sometimes … well, I get to the point where I can't follow one more rule. So I end up doing something like playing hooky from work and going to a baseball game or flirting with a guy in a club or …" she patted her stomach. "Sleeping with a guy that I shouldn't."

He squeezed her hand. "I had a couple of one night stands trying to forget you."

"You did?"

"Yeah. I feel like I've tried everything to get you out of my head," he said. "But you just won't leave."

She didn't say anything else and they exited the park and he led her to the restaurant he'd chosen. It was a pop up Asian fusion place that was run by Alfonso, the first kid he'd been a big brother to. That had been almost ten years ago. Alfonso was an up and coming chef and Hoop was proud of the man that he'd become.

"A pop-up?"

"Yes. Do you mind?"

"No. Not at all. Iona wants us to do something like this leading up to Christmas. She thinks that we can make money by having more than one location. But I'm not really sure how to monetize it."

"Well, I know the chef and he runs this place like a small business. If you'd like, I can introduce you and you can chat with him about it."

That would be a good idea. Hoop didn't want Cici to feel pressured by this date, and their talk as they'd walked over had made him realize he hadn't really thought this through. Granted, Cici was a very different woman than she had been the last time they'd hung out together, but he also hadn't seen her as anything more than a sexy woman he was obsessed with. Her life was complicated and he could easily see himself falling for her. But he'd always promised himself he'd stay single.

He had no idea how a good relationship worked. He'd seen other couples make it work but he'd always known it wasn't for him.

Cici was going to need a man who wanted more than a few months of sex and some friendship when he moved on. And Hoop wasn't too sure he could deliver that. *Hell, he knew he couldn't.*

He led her up the steps of the restaurant where Alfonso's partner, Lulu, was doing the front of house service.

"Hoop. It's been too long since we last saw you," she said, coming over to give him a hug. Lulu was tiny, not even five foot tall. She had long brown hair that she wore in a thick braid down her back. She had her nose pierced with a small sparkling gem and she wore heavy eye make-up that made her look exotic.

"It has been too long. I have been meaning to stop by but the job has been crazy," Hoop said. "This is my friend Cici."

"Hello, Cici. Nice to meet you," Lulu said. "Fonz thought being a lawyer wasn't going to be your thing. Too many office hours."

"He was right, but I do like the work so it's not that bad," Hoop said.

"You sound like me, dude," Alfonso said as he came in from the back of the restaurant. The place was small and could only seat ten customers. There was a couple in the corner and another party of four eating appetizers near the window.

Hoop and Alfonso hugged and when Hoop stepped back he drew Cici closer and introduced her to Alfonso. He thought about how lost he'd been when Pops had stepped into his life and how he'd passed it on by helping out Alfonso when he'd been in the same place.

He kept in touch with both men, and with the other kids he was a big brother to and he liked it. It was enough for him.

But as Cici was talking and he watched Lulu and Alfonso he wondered if he was missing something.

"Ready for dinner? I've got a new dish that is going to blow you away," Alfonso said excitedly.

"I'm ready."

"Me too," Cici said.

Lulu led them to a table and after they were seated and alone, Cici leaned in. "So you do a lot of work with Big Brothers?"

"Yes. It's a good organization," Hoop said.

"I didn't see that side of you," she said.

"We met in a club. You saw the party animal."

"I did," she conceded. "I'm trying to reconcile the two men."

"They aren't two men," he said. "Any more than you are two women."

"You're right. It's just I thought of you as one kind of person."

"What kind is that?"

"I don't know. I mean you're an ex-cop turned attorney, you're a big brother and you like Shakespeare … I guess I just had a one-dimensional image of you."

He didn't know how to respond to that. He wasn't really super comfortable talking about himself and thankfully, Lulu brought over their complimentary appetizers; some spring rolls. They ate and Hoop steered the conversation to safer topics like books and music. They had some things in common.

Though he was never going to understand why women loved Jane Austen as much as they did. Cici made a convincing argument for the appeal of a man with manners. It was a fun night and Hoop wanted to pretend that he could be satisfied with it, but to be honest, Cici had whetted his appetite. He wanted more. *He needed more.*

He knew he was going to ask her out again until he could satisfy the growing need inside of him. He just had to.

Chapter 3

Dinner was delicious and for a while she forgot about everything as they ate and talked about books, movies and what shows they binge-watched on Netflix. He was a sucker for police procedural shows and she favored comic book heroes.

They ordered dessert and as they waited for their dishes to come, he leaned forward. A thick swath of dark hair fell onto his forehead and he pushed it back, making him look more boyish in the dim lighting of the restaurant. He was always serious, so it was interesting to see this other side of him. The light stubble on his jaw did nothing to detract from the attraction Cici felt for him. In fact, she wouldn't mind running her fingers down the line of his jaw. His eyes were blue, not like the sky, more like a grayish blue that she'd seen a few times at dawn. His lips were full and he was easy to make smile.

Life would be so much easier if she'd never met him, Cici thought. Hoop's hair was longer on the top than at the back and a strand fell forward as he took a sip from his water glass. He raised his thick eyebrows at her.

"So tell me about the guy."

The guy.

There wasn't a note of judgment in Hoop's voice. If there had been she would have shut him down and left. But instead there was curiosity and friendliness.

She closed her eyes, wishing she'd skipped dessert and left about two minutes ago. Before he'd gotten around to that.

He was an actor, but not one she'd ever heard of. Though she recalled that he'd been rather loquacious about a pilot he'd shot before coming to Jamaica, but frankly he'd talked a lot and she'd been more focused on the champagne than on what he'd been saying.

"There's not really much to tell," she said.

"His name maybe?" Hoop asked. "Listen, if you don't want to talk about him … then I'll let it go. I'm just curious."

She wasn't keeping the guy a secret so it didn't matter to her, except that she sort of wanted to pretend that it had *never* happened.

"I really don't want to talk about it because this entire thing is not who I usually am. I'm methodical, you know? I plan things out and then act accordingly."

"Why didn't you with him?"

"Because …" she took a sip of her drink and wondered if she should be honest with him, and then realized she had nothing to lose. They weren't dating and probably after tonight he'd start avoiding her so she could just as well tell him without really worrying.

"The truth … is you hurt me that night at Olympus. I thought we had a connection and when you shut me down it brought up all these doubts in myself as a woman. So, when I went to my cousin's wedding and one of the groomsmen was flirting with me—it was flattering. His name is Rich. Rich Maguire. I had too much champagne. He did too and in the morning we both regretted it. I left as quickly as I could."

Hoop fiddled with his fork, turning it over and over in his hands before putting it back down on the table. "I never meant for you to feel like that. I'm sorry, Cici."

"It's okay," she said. "I think it was just Hayley finding someone to share her life with and I don't know. Just sometimes I get distracted by a pair of blue-gray eyes."

"I don't do relationships well," he said. "I ... I grew up in the foster system so I hesitate when things feel ... well, like they could be real. I'm always afraid to believe it. And Garrett is like a brother to me. I didn't want ..."

She put her hand on his. "It's okay. Really."

She didn't want to make Hoop feel bad about that night. If she hadn't gone to the wedding maybe she would have gotten herself out of her funk. But she had and she'd slept with Rich. That was that.

"Is he definitely out of the picture? Or did he just need time to process everything?" Hoop asked.

"He's out. He was, like 'get an abortion, keep the baby, I don't care what you do. I have a fiancée and don't need this'."

"That was pretty harsh," Hoop said. "I wasn't expecting that."

"Me either," she said. "But to be fair we don't know each other at all. And we both had said it was a drunken mistake. I just wanted him to know there was a baby in case it mattered."

"I'm sorry," he said.

"Don't be. I like the idea of raising bean here on my own."

"Bean?"

"Yeah, that's what I've been calling the baby."

"Cute."

"Yes, d non-gender specific."

"Are you going to find out if it's a boy or girl?" Hoop asked.

She rubbed her hand over her stomach. She sort of assumed she'd have a girl. Frankly, she was way better with her own sex than with the opposite one and it seemed like God might want her to succeed at this parenting thing. "Maybe."

The desserts arrived and she looked down at the decadent chocolate lava cake, taking a bite and closing her eyes as she did so. Hayley always said the first bite of chocolate on the tongue was the best. She could tell that they used the same chocolate they did. She let the rich creaminess fill her mouth and then opened her eyes to find Hoop staring at her with an odd expression on his face.

"You okay?"

He nodded and then cleared his throat, stretching his legs out under the table, his foot brushing against hers.

"Um … did you talk to a lawyer about the situation?" he asked, slightly distracted by her touch.

"No. Should I?" she asked. Right now she was busy dealing with morning sickness and trying to figure out herself as a mother. Rich had said he wanted no role in the baby's life and she hadn't thought beyond that fact.

"Yes. I'm not advising you to do so just because family law is what I do, but also from experience. If the Candied Apple & Café continues to grow and you become a millionaire he might suddenly show up in your life again. Also, you want to have some safe guards in place for the child if they ask about the father later," Hoop said. He took a sip of his coffee thoughtfully.

"I hadn't thought of any of that. Actually, I'm still sort of coming to terms with everything," she admitted. "Do you know a good lawyer who does that sort of thing?"

"I do."

"Do I have to guess who it is?" she asked when he didn't elaborate.

He winked at her. "Me. That's what I do. But since we are friends, I will give you the name of one of my colleagues."

"Really? I knew you were a lawyer but you seem more like a criminal defense one."

"Why did you think that?"

"You seem tough and I know you were a cop. What made you want to do family law?"

"Growing up the way I did made me very aware of how complicated family legal matters can be."

She reached across the table and put her hand over his, squeezing it gently. He made that statement so nonchalantly that she almost believed that he didn't really feel anything about it, but there was a note in his voice that gave him away. That made her realize that his past wasn't perfect.

Just like hers.

Both of them had come from families that were less than perfect.

They were closer now than she'd have thought at the beginning of the meal and a part of her didn't regret it at all. Another part of her did. She wasn't too fond of discovering more ways to bond with Hoop.

Hoop hadn't meant to bring up the other guy but frankly he was pissed at himself and Rich for the situation. He should have followed his gut the night they'd met but instead he'd done what he thought was right.

Made the adult decision.

So now he was sitting across from the woman he wanted, listening to her talk baseball stats and getting turned on. And she'd friend zoned him. Probably the smartest choice. He was a man known for his logic, but with Cici that had never been the case.

And that would have to be enough because pressuring a woman into a deeper relationship went totally against the grain. He wasn't about to do it now with Cici.

"I know some people say Derek Jeter is the all-time greatest but if you look at the stats, he's no Babe Ruth or Ty Cobb. It's almost like he's not even playing in the same league. You can't beat those guys who made the sport great. They set standards using equipment that was rougher, heavier, not machined to make the game easier, you know?"

He did know. He also knew that nothing excited him as much as hearing her talk about baseball. There was that passion again that he'd first noticed at the Olympus in February.

Regret didn't taste good with port, he thought.

"Which is why I invited you to the baseball game together," he said. "We could have a really good time."

She smiled and then sighed.

She leaned forward, putting her elbows on the table and resting her head on her left hand. She looked at him from under those heavy brows and thick lashes and he suddenly couldn't really pay attention to anything but the fall of her dark hair against her cheek. Why had he never noticed how pink her lips were before this? Or how kissable her mouth was?

She sat up, leaning forward toward him. "I'm trying to be smart for my baby. I never expected to be a Mom ... not like this and I need to focus on that. And I'm going to be totally honest here, you distract me."

"Well, let's fix that. We need to figure this out," he said. "The more we try to deny it, the more it will grow and then how awkward will getting together with Garrett and Hayley be?"

She shook her head and took another sip of the green tea she'd ordered after dinner. "Nope, it's not going to work. I see where you are going. But we had a shot and now I have this little bean. I can't ..."

"You can. It's not like I'm not a decent guy. You liked me enough to kiss me in Olympus and once again in the cab when I took you home."

She put her mug down on the saucer and gave him a hard look. "But you didn't like me enough. I'm sorry. I'm not trying to be difficult. But you hurt me, Hoop. You made me feel like I wasn't enough. I don't like that. I act stupid when I'm hurt like that."

Her words wounded him but only because he hadn't thought of things from her point-of-view. He had pushed her away. She'd been willing to give him a chance; a real chance, but he'd been a guy.

"I'm an ass."

"Agreed," she said, with a smile. "Just kidding ... you're not an ass. I think you are actually a really nice guy. The kind of man who is responsible and a good friend."

He hadn't thought that he'd hurt her but now it consumed him. Made him realize how arrogant he'd been in thinking he could come back to her. He owed her. He needed to show her she wasn't the problem. That they could, at the very least, be friends. "Let me be a friend to you, Cici. Let me prove I can be a good friend to you."

She shook her head. "Ugh. You're not going to take no for an answer, are you?"

"Nope. Sorry, it's not in my programming to give up on something that means a lot to me."

"And I mean a lot to you?" she asked. "We don't really know each other."

"I know. But I think we could be good friends," he said. At least to start out with. She was having a baby and he knew how fragile families were. He'd gone into family law because he wanted to help bring people together.

"Okay. I'll go to a baseball game with you and then we can see what happens next."

Hoop was at her door early for their date. She almost didn't answer it but she had decided as soon as she'd found out about her little bean that she wasn't going to run away any more. It was a baseball game. No big deal, right?

She opened the door and he stood there wearing a faded Yankees t-shirt and holding his glove loosely in one hand. His jeans were faded too and clung to his thighs.

She sighed. He was too good looking. It would have been nice if his nose had been broken and hadn't healed properly or maybe if he had a little bit of a beer belly. But no.

"You okay?"

"What? Yes, sorry about that," she said. She pulled the door closed behind her and locked it.

"What are you wearing?"

"My Red Sox shirt."

"I can see that, why?"

"I'm a Red Sox fan," she said. "I grew up in Connecticut."

"This is going to be awkward," he said, smiling.

"More awkward than me being pregnant?" she asked with a grin. She had decided to own it. She'd been hiding the pregnancy from her friends and family because she'd been uncomfortable and embarrassed but talking with Hoop the other night at dinner had helped her get clarity. She had decided to have the baby and she was going to figure out how to be the best damn mother she could be.

He threw his head back and laughed. She smiled, realizing just how long it had been since she'd heard him laugh. It had been that night in the club. Pre-pregnancy.

"Fair point. I have season tickets," he said. "You're going to be sitting in the heart of the Yankee Country."

"I'm tougher than I look," she said. "Plus, my team is going to whip yours and I'm prepared to be a generous winner."

They took the subway to Yankee Stadium and Cici got a few comments on the way. There were Red Sox fans on the subway as well. But she and Hoop both ignored them.

"Maybe this wasn't the best idea for a first date," Hoop said. "But you're the first girl I've met in a long time that actually loves baseball."

"This isn't technically a date," she said, trying to keep it clear to herself and him that they were just friends. "And that can't be true. Other women love the sport."

"They still love Derek Jeter even though he's retired, but you know stats," he said.

"I'm a numbers girl," Cici said, as they walked into the stadium and past a row of food vendors. The smells were intense and she'd never wanted a hot dog and beer as badly. She knew the beer was out but a hotdog with mustard and onions. That would be … perfection.

She suspected it was pregnancy but she also knew she wanted a distraction. Baseball and men. She should have known better than to combine the two. It was her weakness.

"Want a hot dog?" she asked.

"I'd rather know why you love baseball," Hoop replied, but he made his way to the vendor closest to them and got in line. "I know a lot of people who are good with numbers who don't have a passion for the game."

"That's personal."

"It's how we are going to get to know one another better," Hoop said.

"Really?" she asked. But she remembered the other night and how talking with him about the uncomfortable stuff had helped.

"Yes," he said. "What do you want on your dog?"

"Mustard and onions," she said.

"Drink?"

Beer. But she couldn't. Her grandmother talked about how she'd drank and smoked while she'd been pregnant with Cici's mom, to which Cici's mom always quipped "look how normal I am", but Cici wasn't taking any chances.

"I'll have a soda."

"Wait for me over there?" he asked, gesturing to a spot where the crowds were thin.

She walked over there, noting that a cool breeze blew up from the opening. She watched Hoop. He was tall and handsome but more than that he seemed to have a kind soul. She had never had a good radar with men. She knew this. And given that her first impression of him had been dead wrong, she was afraid to trust her instincts where he was concerned.

She'd liked him, he'd rejected her, she had acted impulsively. She rubbed her hands over her lower stomach where her little bean was nestled.

He came over with their food and led the way up to their seats. She ignored some of the jeers she got as they sat down. She just smiled and ate her hotdog. Hayley had made her some kale chips which Cici dug out of her bag. Hayley wanted her to eat healthily. Iona was convinced that Cici wasn't getting enough exercise and had taken to stopping by her apartment every morning before work to walk through Central Park with her.

She sighed, offering a kale chip to Hoop.

"No way. It's bad enough I'm sitting with a Red Sox fan, I'm not eating pretend chips."

"They taste better than you might think," she said.

"That's because nothing really tastes like cardboard," he said, taking a swallow of his beer. "This is nice."

So many times she'd felt alone in life but Hayley and Iona were sisters of the heart. She'd gotten lucky one of her exes had dated all three of them at the same time. Without him she would never have met Iona or Hayley and started the Candied Apple & Café. She tried not to dwell on the fact that something good had come out of her bad taste in men.

"It is nice," she said. But she knew she wasn't talking about the weather or even about the game that was about to start. She was slowly coming to find that Hoop wasn't like the other guys she'd known. He was different.

It had been hard to see at first because of his floppy hair and the way his jeans hugged his ass, but there was more to Hoop than his sexy smile and the butterflies he made her feel. He was a nice guy. A good guy. Someone she had to get to know more.

Chapter 4

At the bottom of the fifth, the Red Sox were up by two and Cici wasn't feeling the love from the others around her. Except for Hoop who couldn't stop smiling at her.

She stood up to cheer.

"Cici."

"Yes?"

He didn't say another word, just lowered his head and their lips brushed. There was that electric buzz that went from her lips through her entire body. She closed her eyes and felt the brush of his breath over her lips before he kissed her. He pushed his tongue into her mouth with a gentle caress and she pulled him closer, going up on her tiptoes to deepen the embrace.

He smelled of summer. Sunshine and beer and hotdogs. And some scent that was just Hoop. He held her close and she felt like she wasn't alone.

Damn.

She wanted to pull him closer and take more from him. Take everything that he had to give her and keep it. But she wasn't sure that was possible.

He was strong, so she wanted to borrow his strength. She

wanted to figure out how he was able to always be that way when she'd been faking for too long.

He kept his hands on her face, his touch light and she held onto his waist as he angled his head and broke the kiss. He looked down at her and she looked up at him and realized that no matter what she was trying to convince herself of, she wanted Hoop.

Her blood was pounding a little heavier through her veins, her skin felt so sensitized that when he skimmed his fingers down the side of her neck, goose bumps spread down her arm.

She pulled back and felt the hotdog and kale chips she'd eaten earlier start making their way back up. Damn.

"Sorry," she said, covering her mouth with her hand.

She swallowed and reached for her bottle of water. Her "morning" sickness wasn't going away. She tried to bolt down the aisle but not everyone was quick to move.

"I'm going to be sick," she yelled, and if she wasn't feeling so bad she would have laughed at how quickly the Yankee's fans moved out of her way. She barely made it to the restroom before she threw up everything she'd eaten that day.

Her stomach wasn't happy just emptying the contents but added acid and bile to the mix. When she was finally finished heaving, she went to the sink to rinse her face and wash out her mouth. She hadn't realized how much she hated throwing up. But to be honest, until her pregnancy, it had been limited to some mornings in college when she'd drunk too much the night before.

This was different. She felt weak and wanted to just curl in a ball and have her mom bring her warm 7-Up and crackers. But she knew that wasn't going to happen. She had to go back to her seat and rejoin Hoop. She patted her pocket and realized she'd left her phone and bag in the stadium.

"Bean, you are torturing me," she said.

She walked out of the restroom and found Hoop standing against the cement wall across from the exit. He had her purse in one hand and a bottle of water in the other. He had his legs crossed at the ankles and gave her a tentative smile when he saw her.

"Some of the other fans thought you had it coming for cheering so loudly," he said. "A few unkind ones suggested it might have been my kiss."

"It definitely wasn't your kiss," she said, trying to smile. Her voice sounded funny and raw from being sick and he pushed away from the wall and walked over to her, holding out the bottle of water. She took a swallow. He handed her a piece of minty gum and she took it. He was very thoughtful and thorough.

How could she think about getting involved with Hoop? Would he even want to after that?

Being sick was just the beginning. Her body was going to change and if the chapters she'd skipped ahead to read in her pregnancy book were any indication, some of the stuff was not going to be pleasant.

"I'm sorry."

"Why?"

"I can't do this to you. You don't want to be friends with a pregnant lady, Hoop. I've read the books and it's just going to get worse."

He put his hand on the back of her neck and rubbed in a soft circular motion. "Too late. I'm not going to let you keep backing away. We've already decided to give this a try."

"We did?" she asked. She didn't think they'd done that but she wasn't ready to walk away from him yet.

"And you don't strike me as someone who backs down. I mean I saw you cheering on your team in enemy country."

She smiled, even though she didn't want to. And then wondered why she didn't want to. Did she have to punish herself because she'd made a mistake with this man? Was that why she was trying so hard to find any reason not to be with him.

She leaned forward, putting her forehead on his chest and her arms around his waist. She could tell she startled him because his hand dropped to his side and then he wrapped his arms around her.

She held him and didn't say anything. Just took comfort from this man who she really didn't know what to do with. And right now, as crappy as she was feeling, she didn't want to have to figure it out or worry about the future. She just needed … Hoop.

She lifted her head, staring up into those brilliant blue eyes of his and he put his hands on her head, tucked the long strand of her bangs back behind her ear.

He tangled their fingers together and turned so they were facing the exit. "Let's go."

"Go where?"

"Somewhere we can be alone," he said.

She wanted to be the woman she saw when he looked at her. Someone who was strong. Strong enough to make the right choices and to own up to the world if she didn't.

They'd caught a cab to Red Roosters in Harlem because Cici was hungry and somehow taking her back to his place had bad idea written all over it. Kissing her had changed something inside of him. Watching her run away to be sick had been a pretty clear reminder of her circumstances.

She needed a friend and he'd offered.

It wasn't one he'd made lightly though. His hormones were doing their damnedest to convince him that friends with benefits was a good idea, but he knew she needed just a friend. She was on her own with the baby. And he knew how fragile that could be. He'd seen it as an adult and lived through it as a child.

And she had seemed to lose some of her glow after she'd gotten sick. Who could blame her? So, he sat in a corner booth across from her and asked her about baseball.

"You are a crazy massive fan of baseball," he said, taking a sip of his sweet tea. He needed something to cool him down but it wasn't the heat in the city that had him on fire. It was Cici.

40

Her hair kept curling around her face and she tucked the same strand behind her ear repeatedly. That strand. It had been soft and silky to the touch. Just like her lips. He wanted to kiss her again but he was being cool. She'd worn contacts today and he noticed how pretty her eyes were.

But he was honoring her desire for them to be friends. Plus, he knew she needed more from him than just full on guy hormones. She needed comfort and to feel normal. He'd not been around pregnant women much. One of his sisters at the Fillions' foster home had a baby last year but she lived in Florida now with her husband so he hadn't seen her while she'd been expecting.

Just from watching Cici, he noticed how much it drained her. She'd been pale when she'd come out of the bathroom and shaken. The way she'd hugged him ... she needed him.

No one had ever really needed him. He volunteered, of course, and he knew the kids he was a big brother to really appreciated it, but he had never felt as needed with them as he had with Cici this afternoon. This had felt more personal.

"I am a pretty intense fan when it comes to the Red Sox," she admitted. "One year I went to spring training."

"Just one year?" he asked with a wink. "How can you call yourself a massive fan?"

"Alright smarty, how many spring training games have you been to?" she asked.

"One. And that was just because my sister had a new baby and we all went to Florida," he explained.

"Sister? I thought you were adopted. Did your parents ... what happened with your parents?" she asked, reaching onto his plate and stealing a fry.

"Lisa is my sister but we aren't biological siblings. She and I grew up in the same home ... the Fillions. Did I tell you about them?"

"No. What happened to your folks?" she asked. "If I'm being

41

too nosey just tell me to mind my own business. I think it's a side effect of hanging out with Iona all the time."

He rubbed his hand over his chest. His real parents. People always wanted to know about them. And frankly, he wanted to as well. "I have no idea. Near as anyone can figure, my mom was a teenager who gave birth ..." he shrugged, "somewhere ... and then dropped me off at the hospital and kept on trucking. Never gave me a name or anything."

She reached across the table and took his hand in hers. She laced their fingers together and she squeezed gently. "I'm sorry. I never knew my dad either, so I can sort of understand not knowing."

"It's more than that," he admitted. But they were on a date and he didn't want to get into how he'd felt unworthy for so many years. He was better now; he knew that the problem was hers and not anything to do with him. But there were times when he wished he could meet her and show her what she'd walked away from.

"I can't even begin to imagine," she said. "How did you get your name?"

"The center she dropped me off at was on Hooper Street," he said. "And one of the nurses thought I looked like a Jason. They had to fill in the paperwork. When I was a cop I went to investigate and found out about all the legalities involved. It's how I decided to switch to being a lawyer."

He took another sip of his sweet tea but it tasted too cloying now and he set it aside. Talking about his past always left him feeling ... well, odd. That was the only word for it.

"I've reached out to one of my coworkers about your case and if you have time next week, I'd love for you to stop by the office and meet with her. Then you can get the paperwork started to send them to your ... I don't know what to call him."

Cici blushed. "Baby daddy? Sperm donor?"

"No. That's not it," he said. "Mr. Maguire."

"Once he signs the papers then you'll be protected and to be honest, he will be too. That way you can't go back to him and demand anything from him."

"I would never do that," Cici said.

"I know. But it will give him peace of mind and make him more amenable to signing the papers," Hoop said. He'd handled a lot of cases like hers and knew that having a binding contract wasn't always enough but it gave each party some peace of mind. He wanted to make sure that Cici was protected.

"Good. I just want that done," she said. "I think once this is settled, well I can really start to figure out things for the baby."

"Like what?" he asked. He didn't know what a child would need or what a single mom would. Seeing Cici on her own made him wonder if his own mother had been like this. Did she have a friend to talk to? He'd never know. He knew that but it stirred questions all the same.

"Like the nursery colors and theme … and then I have to find a preschool and get on the waiting list," she said.

"You haven't even given birth yet," he said, but he knew from one of his co-workers who was struggling to get their kids into the right school how hard it was.

"You have no idea about all the things that I have to decide," she said.

"On your own?" he asked softly.

"I haven't told my mom and stepdad yet. I mean Hayley and Iona have been great but this kind of thing is definitely something I have to figure out."

"I can ask around at my office and get a list of the best schools," he said. "Maybe see if someone can write a letter of recommendation for you."

"You'd do that?" she asked.

"Yes. We're friends. You're going to need lots of them," he said. She took another sip of her water, finally getting full. She leaned back against the seat and watched Hoop. The kiss … she'd been ignoring it since they'd left the ballpark because she wanted to focus on friendship but he'd stirred something deep inside of her. Something she thought would be dormant now that she was expecting. And that her life was up in the air.

But it wasn't.

"You okay?"

"Yes," she said, wishing he hadn't caught her staring at him. "I was just thinking how I need to build up a network of other parents. I remember when I was young, before my mom met Steven, my stepdad, how alone we were."

"That's not going to happen to you," he said.

"No, it's not. I always thought when I had a kid I'd be more sensible about the planning. My dad was in special forces and so his job was dangerous … I mean I know they couldn't have guessed he'd be killed but I just thought, if I was smart about it, then I could do it right."

"Right?" he asked. "I'm not sure I'm following."

"Just that I'd find a guy and have kids with him and we'd both raise them. No divorce or risky jobs. That way the kids could grow up in a house where they knew they were loved."

Cici realized how that sounded. That maybe she'd said too much. "Sorry about that. I think all the food is going to my head. This place is great."

He crossed his arms over his chest, arching one eyebrow over at her. "It is great. Was that your way of saying you'd had enough of the conversation?"

"Yes," she said. She didn't want to think about the fact that her child was going to want to know who their father was at some point. And she'd have to tell them about Rich not wanting to be a part of their life. God, that was going to be hard. When she met with Hoop's lawyer friend maybe she'd ask if there was a provision they could put in just in case the child wanted to meet him.

"Fair enough," he said. "What do you want to do now?"

"I think I'm ready to head home," she said. She had a lot to think about. And she wanted to try to forget the kiss they'd shared. It had been incredible. "The game was a lot of fun. I wish I hadn't gotten sick."

"Me too. But that's to be expected. You seem better now," he said. "I'm glad. Do you know how long morning sickness lasts? I think with my sister she had it for four months."

"The book said each expectant mother is different," Cici said. She'd gone to a few websites as well and her doctor had told her once she relaxed and learned to listen to the changes in her body it would help. "I really hope it ends soon."

"I bet," he said. He signaled the waiter for the bill.

She reached for her wallet and he cleared his throat.

"What?"

"I know you are not going to try to pay for lunch," he said.

"What if I was?" she asked. She always paid her own way. She had already calculated the cost of her portion and the tip.

"It's a date, Cici. That means lunch is on me."

"It's the twenty-first century, Hoop, a woman can pay," she said, though she knew she was needling him. She thought it was nice when a guy paid after asking her out.

"Well I'm old fashioned that way," he said.

"What other ways are you old fashioned?" she asked. "You wanted to pick me up at my place. That sort of thing?"

"I guess. Just seems polite to pick you up from your place. You know how I told you I was in trouble a lot as a teenager?"

"Yes."

"Well I spent a lot of time reading books and I picked up some things that … I don't know, I guess resonated with the kind of man I wanted to be. You know Mr. Fillion, my pops, influenced me when I got to their house but before that I had to find my own male role model."

She wanted to find the little boy inside of him and give him a hug. He'd struggled growing up and she reminded herself that she didn't want her child to have to go through that. "Is that why you volunteer with Big Brother?"

"Partially. We all need to know we have someone to reach out to," he said, handing his credit card to the waiter.

She waited until the waiter had gone because not everything that was said between them needed a witness. And she liked letting him stew for a few minutes.

"But we can talk more about that on our next date," he said.

"What makes you think we'll have a second date?"

"This one went pretty well," he said, "And you like me."

He held his hand out to help her from the bench and she shook her head as she followed him out the door. She did like him.

Chapter 5

Three days later and she still hadn't really heard from Hoop. She'd gone to his offices and met the lawyer he'd recommended and had sort of hoped to see him there. But he hadn't been. In retrospect she got that. Her legal matter wasn't something that he should be involved in.

He was giving her space … letting her set the tone of their relationship. He had suggested a second date though.

And…

Nothing.

She had her new routine … work, get sick, worry about how to tell her parents she was pregnant. She knew her stepdad would be disappointed but then she felt like she hadn't done anything to please him in years.

She rubbed the back of her neck and sat back in her chair, staring at the screen on her large monitor and hoping for an answer. She wanted to make a decision matrix, though she hadn't used one since deciding to go in with Iona and Hayley to open the Candied Apple & Café.

Her door, which had been shut, but not tightly closed, was nudged open and the jingle of Lucy's collar alerted her to the fact that Hayley's rescue dachshund was on the move. She glanced to her left and saw the small dog looking up at her, tail wagging.

"What do you want?" she asked in the singsong voice she always used with kids and pets.

The dog went up on her back legs and motioned with her front paws up and down. Cici shook her head and turned her chair to the little dog who went down on all fours, wagging her tale as she inched closer to Cici's feet.

Cici picked Lucy up and the dog put her front paws on Cici's chest, licking her chin. She rubbed her hands up and down the dog's back, petting her.

If only it were as easy to make people this happy.

Her message app on the computer pinged and she reached around the dog to click on the icon to open it up. Lucy circled three times and then plunked down on Cici's lap.

The message was a group text from Iona to her and Hayley.

Iona: *Lunch, Bryant Park, 30 minutes. No excuses.*

Hayley: *I need 45 minutes to finish the candy I'm working on.*

Cici: *I can come early. Lucy is with me. Okay to bring her?*

Hayley: *So that's where that little scamp got to. She was sleeping in her bed.*

Iona: *So see you in 30, Cici?*

Cici: *Yes.*

She closed the text app and put her computer in sleep mode before going to collect Lucy's leash, collapsible water bowl and treats from Hayley.

"I'm so jealous that you are leaving now," Hayley said. "I need a break."

"You okay?"

Hayley shrugged. Her blonde hair was now hitting the back of her neck and she'd tucked it behind her ear. "I'm grumpy today."

"Why?"

"I'll tell you at lunch. Don't talk too much until I get there," Hayley said, hugging her.

"We won't," Cici promised.

She left the shop from the back and walked up the alley to Fifth Avenue. She stopped for a minute, tipping her head back to look at the buildings. The walk to Bryant Park from their Fifth Avenue location would take about twenty-five minutes, so she wasn't in too much of a hurry. She started up Fifth to Madison Square Park. The summery day was warm and being out and walking was doing wonders for her state of mind. She swapped her glasses for prescription sunglasses. Lucy generated a lot of smiles from passersby and the little dog always stopped to allow anyone who showed an interest in her to pet her. At the park, Cici gave her a little bit of water while she drank from the bottle of strawberry infused water she had in her bag.

She took a deep breath. The City smelled … well, like a big city. Here in the park it was fragrant with lush greenery but the underlying smell of industry was in the air as well. She stood there and realized how much time she'd spent worrying over the last few months and that she should let it go.

She needed to stop thinking she could change anything. She never had been able to. She wasn't going to be the person who made the "right choices" whatever they were, because that wasn't who she was. She followed her gut and that had sometimes led her into trouble but it had also resulted in some of her best choices. The Candied Apple & Café was one. This baby was going to be another one.

Lucy tugged on her leash, ready to start moving again, and Cici put the cap tightly on her bottle and dropped it back in her bag.

She continued up Fifth, realizing that her steps were a little bouncier. Being herself was probably the one thing she'd always been good at. In school, when it wasn't cool to be good at math, she'd ignored the other kids and just did her thing. When other girls didn't like baseball the way she did and thought it was nerdy that she knew the stats … well, screw them. Somehow finding out she was pregnant with one man's baby while still crushing on another one had thrown her.

She'd forgotten who she was.

And being a mom didn't have to mean losing herself.

She couldn't let it mean that. She was all this little bean of hers was going to have. Well and some aunties in Hayley and Iona, and of course, her parents. Her stepdad and mom might not be excited about how she got pregnant but she knew they'd love and welcome her baby.

What about Rich's family? She hadn't met them at the wedding but her cousin had mentioned he came from a wealthy family. Would they want to be part of the baby's life? And exactly how would that conversation go?

Hey, you don't know me but I hooked up with your son at a wedding and now I'm carrying your grandchild?

Uh, not so much.

She'd worry about that later.

All of a sudden it hit her … she had been wearing a mantle of blame.

Damn.

She was ashamed of herself.

She hadn't admitted it before now.

She stopped at the corner of Fifth and stepped out of the flow of traffic, leaning against a building as the truth of that thought echoed in her mind.

She wrapped her arms around her stomach. She wasn't going to be ashamed of her baby.

Lucy looked up at her and whined in a way that Cici thought sounded like a question.

"I'm okay," she said.

And as she continued walking toward Bryant Park she realized that she *was* okay. Now that she knew the cause of her moods she could face it and deal with it head on.

*

Hoop leaned back in his chair and glanced out of his window, which afforded him a view of the skyscraper building next door. It was hot and the air conditioning in the building was working overtime to keep them all comfortable. He'd like to say that he was distracted by the heat but the truth was Cici was on his mind.

He'd give her the space she needed. And to be honest, that he needed. Getting involved with her was complicated. Not least by the fact that he didn't do well with relationships.

He didn't need a therapist to tell him that it was rooted in his nomadic childhood. But there was a part of him that insisted everything was temporary. And a baby deserved stability. Permanence. The things that Hoop felt inadequate to bring to the table.

There was a knock at the door.

"Come in," he said.

The door opened and he saw his boss, Martin Reynolds, standing there. Martin was sixty but looked more like forty. He worked out twice a day in the office gym and prided himself on being healthy.

"Got a minute?" Martin asked. His boss wore a Hugo Boss suit and kept his salt-and-pepper hair neatly trimmed. He'd made his reputation by settling a huge custody case in the 80s involving two warring billionaires. Hoop admired Martin and respected him.

And he wondered why he was here in his office. He'd had two conversations with Martin before and they'd both taken place in the executive boardroom on the twentieth floor. None of the partners had ever come to his office before.

"I have about ten," Hoop said. "I have a client meeting in thirty minutes."

"Perfect," Martin said, coming into the room and taking a seat in the guest chair. He sat down, loosely crossing his legs and leaned back in his chair.

That old fear. The one that said that everything in his life was temporary reared its head and he started to sweat as he realized his boss might be in here to deliver bad news. His last two cases had brought the firm a nice profit and had pleased his clients. But maybe he hadn't been working hard enough.

"Though you've been at this office for only two years, we've all been impressed with your work ethic and the cases you've handled," Martin said.

"Thank you, sir," Hoop said. "I love my work."

"I thought so," Martin replied with a smile. "You remind me a bit of myself."

"How so?" he asked, because he didn't see much in Martin's life that resembled his.

"I didn't come to law as a first choice either."

"Were you a cop?" Hoop asked. It was hard to imagine Martin as a cop but he was tough and had a strong sense of justice.

Martin gave a laugh. "Not at all. I was a salesman. Worked for a large retail chain in their corporate headquarters in the garment district."

"Wow. That's a big change," Hoop said.

"Does everyone say that to you?" Martin asked.

"They do," Hoop admitted.

"Do you feel like it was an epic decision?" Martin asked, leaning forward.

Hoop shook his head. "For me, this is more like finding the career I was meant to have. I loved aspects of being a cop but after the newness of the job wore off, most mornings I dreaded getting up and going to work."

"How do you feel about coming here every day?" Martin asked.

"I love it," Hoop said. It hadn't taken him long to realize he'd found the calling he'd been searching for in family law. His mom always said he'd find it one day but Hoop had doubted her. There were so many questions about where he came from and who he truly was that he'd struggled and would never have chosen this profession, but having stumbled into it, there was a certain rightness to where he was.

"Good. I'm very glad to hear that. Jameson is retiring at the end of the year and all of the partners are looking for candidates to fill his role, which will leave an opening for a junior partner. I'd like you to be my junior partner candidate, Hoop. Are you interested?"

"Yes," he said, without even thinking. "I won't let you down."

"I'm sure you won't. Have your assistant get in touch with mine and schedule weekly check in meetings for us."

"Yes, sir," Hoop said excitedly.

"What does your caseload look like right now?" Martin asked.

"Full but not too heavy," Hoop said. He had about eighty hours a week of work but he wanted the junior partnership enough to sacrifice and do whatever was needed to make it happen. He hadn't thought that he'd have this opportunity so quickly.

"I want to start introducing you to some of our biggest clients and let you work with me on some of the cases so that you can raise your profile within the company. I will copy you in on the cases and have my assistant bring you the files you need to review."

"Sounds great," Hoop said.

"Glad to hear it," Martin replied. "I think that's my time up. I'd like our weekly meetings to be on Monday."

"I'll let Abby know," Hoop said, mentioning his administrative assistant by name.

"It's going to be hard work," Martin said, standing. "But I'm confident you are up for it."

Martin left the room and Hoop jumped out of his chair. *Junior partner!*

He did a fist pump and then a little dance around his desk as his door opened. He stopped mid hip shake to see Abby standing in the doorway.

"So ... Mr. Reynolds said you needed me to set up some appointments."

"I am. You're looking at a candidate for junior partner," Hoop said.

Abby closed the door behind her and walked over to give him a high five. "That's going to be longer hours for us."

"It will. Can you handle it?" he asked. But he knew she could. Abby and he made a good team.

Abby nodded. "Definitely. What's first?"

"I need you to get me on Martin's schedule for weekly one-on-one meetings and his admin … what's her name?"

"Kelscy."

"Thanks, Abby," Hoop said, tucking the name away. He'd need it. "His office will be sending down some files of cases that I need to get up to speed on. I'd like you to build time into my schedule to get caught up on those."

"Got it, boss. Your next appointment is running five minutes late," Abby said, handing him a folder and then turning and leaving his office.

He knew that it would take a lot of hard work to get the job but he was willing to do it. He had an extra five minutes so he picked up his office phone and dialed his parents' house. They'd both be at work so he got the machine.

"Mom, Pops. It's Hoop. I'm a candidate for junior partner. Just thought you'd like to know. Love you."

The Candied Apple & Café had a line out the front door as Cici and Hayley returned from lunch.

"I'd say your new flavors are a hit," Cici said as they approached.

"I guess so. I think making our most popular truffles into milkshakes is also helping draw the crowds. It is so hot today," Hayley added. She linked her free arm through Cici's and stopped walking. Lucy promptly trotted back to Hayley's side, standing up on her back legs to look up at her owner.

"Can you believe this?" Hayley asked. "It seems like just

yesterday we were all sitting in Sant Ambroeus drinking espresso and talking about pooling our skills."

She remembered it. They had all been working for others and not really happy in their careers. Cici had been tired of working in a large accounting department in her cubicle all day. As much as she loved numbers there had been something soul-sucking about the entire environment. Leaving that job had seemed risky at the time but she didn't regret it.

How could she when they'd made such a big success of the Candied Apple & Café? Having the baby would be the same, she thought.

"A part of me wants to be all like, of course I believe it. *Girl power!* But damn, this is bigger than we dreamed," Cici said.

"It is," Hayley agreed. "I kind of want to just stand here and enjoy the scene."

"Me too, but Jo will kill us if we don't do a little video for social media," Cici said.

"Want me to do it?" Hayley asked.

Cici did. But Hayley was incredibly shy and really hated doing any sort of media for the store. "Nah, I got this. Actually, how do I look?"

"Gorgeous as usual."

"I'm sure I look sweaty from our walk," Cici said.

Hayley pulled a bottle of facial hydrating spray from her bag and gave Cici a quick spritz before doing her own face. "Really, I hate to sound like a weirdo but you are glowing. I guess it's those baby hormones making your skin radiant, I'm jealous."

"Uh, don't be, you have a great fiancé. I think if you said you wanted a baby …"

"Stop. Don't say another word. I'm still getting used to living with Garrett and being a couple. I think we need time before we add to our family."

"I wasn't pressuring you," Cici said. Though a part of her sort of wished that Hayley would get pregnant so they could be new moms together.

"I know. It's just sometimes everything with Garrett seems like it is moving too quickly. I like to plan."

"I get it," Cici said. "Wouldn't life be easier if we could plot our personal lives the way we do the Candied Apple & Café?"

"It would," Hayley said with a laugh. "Do you want me to video you talking to the customers?"

"Back to business," Cici said. "No, I'm going to get them chatting and do a little selfie intro … actually let's do it together."

"Uh, what?"

"You don't have to talk to anyone but my cell phone," Cici said.

She extended her arm and hit the reverse camera button. Hayley was right, her skin did look nice. Both she and Hayley made faces at themselves in the selfie camera and Cici hugged her friend with her free arm.

"I'm so glad we're friends."

"Me too."

"Okay, ready? I'll start and then throw it to you. I'm going to say we're here in front of the shop and then ask you to talk about the new flavors and the shakes."

"I'm ready. I could talk about chocolate all day."

"I know. I spend most of my days with you."

"Brat."

"Takes one to know one," Cici said. "Recording in three, two, one …"

Cici recorded herself and Hayley chatting and then Hayley took Lucy and went down the alley entrance way to the kitchen while Cici talked to the customers waiting in line. Since Valentine's Day and the introduction of the love box, a lot of folks she talked to informed her that they had made rituals of getting the new season sampler with their lovers.

Cici felt a pang as she listened to their stories. She wanted someone to share her life with. Not a guy who she'd friend zoned, who seemed content to stay there.

She rubbed the back of her neck, reminded herself that she didn't need a man to complete her. But there was a longing inside of her she couldn't deny. She wanted someone that she had little rituals with.

It wasn't like she couldn't eat chocolate. Heck, she did that daily with her friends. She walked into the shop, felt the cooling of the air conditioning and waved at Carolyn as she walked through the retail section then into the café and back to her office.

She sat in her chair, plugging her phone in to download the videos and as she saw herself and Hayley she realized that she had a good life. The pangs of longing she felt for a man, they would pass. She was building the life she'd always dreamed of.

She had a successful business and a lovely apartment in the city and soon she'd have her little bean.

She patted her stomach and tried to feel some Zen connection to her baby. She'd read that some mothers did, but she felt nothing. That worried her.

She had spent so much time thinking of the fallout maybe she had missed out on bonding with the baby.

She leaned forward, resting her head on her desk.

No, she mentally reprimanded herself. She wasn't going to start feeling bad about anything.

She was the best damned mom this little bean could have and she was going to start acting like it.

Chapter 6

Everyone in the working world looked forward to the weekend. So did she ... well, that wasn't true. She'd always hated the weekends. Even as a kid she'd wanted to be at school. Be busy. Doing something that would keep her from home.

Her mom did her best but it had been awkward once the twins had been born. She'd felt out of place and in the way.

Her stepdad ... well, to give Steve his props, he'd tried. He'd never been mean to her, he wasn't a creep the way some stepdads could be. He just hadn't ... hadn't been her dad. It had been sobering when she'd turned thirteen and realized it. Until that point she'd been an only child. And it had been the three of them. She'd always called Steve "dad" because her daddy had been killed in action serving his country. But that summer her mom had gotten pregnant with the twins. She and Steve had done their usual summer stuff; baseball, making ice cream on the back porch, getting the twins' room ready and then the boys had been born.

And everything had changed.

She rubbed her hand over the back of her neck and got up from the couch where she'd been half-heartedly watching the Food Network. Hayley was always asking Cici for ideas on flavor combinations and to be honest, she didn't have an "adventurous" palate so she watched cooking shows to help develop it.

But this morning her heart wasn't in it.

Her mind was on Hoop and the thought that it wouldn't be fair to her child or to him to start anything. Even friendship.

The reality was … well, she'd lived with a man who'd changed in subtle ways. And Steve was a great guy who'd had seven years of being her dad under his belt before his biological sons were born.

Cici knew that there was a difference between a stepchild and a biological one. She'd experienced it first hand and she'd promised herself she'd never put a child of hers in that situation.

She had always sort of thought she'd make the right choice. Have kids with one guy and if he died like her dad had, Cici had promised herself she'd never remarry. But instead she was starting out alone.

She realized she was crying.

Pregnancy hormones, she thought.

She had to get out of this place; this luxury apartment that she'd chosen and carefully decorated to show herself how far she'd come. But this morning it felt like a cage she'd made for herself. A life that wasn't really hers.

She went into her bedroom and changed out of her nightgown into a pair of khaki shorts and a flowing sleeveless top, put on a pair of Vans and then grabbed her sunglasses. She was going to walk until she stopped feeling. Until something nudged her hard enough to make her snap out of the mood she'd fallen into.

She grabbed her purse and double-checked that her American Express was in there. Nothing like a little retail therapy to cure the blues.

She opened the door and walked resolutely toward the elevator, waiting for it to come up.

When the doors opened she felt a twinge of excitement that she quickly quelled.

"Hoop."

"Cici, I'd hoped to surprise you, but it seems you're on your way out," Hoop said.

He wore a pair of jeans and a tee shirt that had a dinosaur holding a puppy on it. The image was random and made her wonder why he wore it. But it hugged the curves of his chest and he smelled good. Like a fresh summery day. That damned after-shave of his.

She closed her eyes and then opened them. She wasn't doing this. They'd said friends and that was all they'd be. One kiss wasn't going to change that. And at the end of the day she wasn't going to fall into a relationship that would have a devastating effect on her child. Even if it wasn't outright obvious to anyone else.

"What's up? I am heading out for a little retail therapy," she said, with a smile, stepping into the elevator car.

He followed her, reaching around her to push the button for the lobby. His arm brushed her shoulder and shivered with aware-ness. She had read in her pregnancy book that her sex drive might increase and honestly, there couldn't be a worse time for it to intensify. She watched him. Watched his mouth as he spoke, not listening to his words, just remembering how smooth and soft his lips had been.

He knew how to kiss and she remembered how good he'd tasted. How could a man taste *so* good? None of the other guys she'd dated had tasted this good. Why Hoop?

"So, what do you think?" he asked as the doors opened and he gestured for her to lead the way into the lobby.

"About what?"

"Weren't you listening to me?"

"Sort of. But with this pregnancy sometimes my mind drifts," she admitted. She'd read about that in the book too. And for once it was the perfect excuse.

"I asked if you wanted to join me and Alfonso and his girl-friend this afternoon. We are taking my boat out in the harbor.

Alfonso's in charge of food, we thought we'd have a picnic on the boat."

She looked at him and thought about how she wanted to get him out of her head. Get away from the past and find the future and she realized that she needed to figure out the now first. But for today she wanted to just stop thinking and analyzing. Her greatest strength was turning into a cross she didn't want to carry. She needed some distance from all of the pros and cons. And it was June. A summer's day out on a boat … who could resist that?

Not her.

"I'd love it. But I'll bring dessert. I work for one of the best chocolate shops in the city. It would be a sin for me not to bring the dessert."

"That sounds absolutely perfect. We're not going until two, so if you want some company, I'll carry your bags while you shop."

When Hoop turned seven he'd entered his fifth foster home in as many years. He was starting to get used to moving and because of his personality he liked the transient nature of his life. He was not one of the troublemakers or one of the kids who were immediately adopted. He was normal. Average.

As he followed Cici into Bonpoint, a trendy upmarket children's clothing shop, he contemplated that being average wasn't a bad thing. She held up a small white bit of cloth that would be safe for either sex.

Hoop suddenly realized what he was getting into. He should walk away. It wasn't like she would be surprised. He'd said they'd be friends but in the back of his mind, he'd thought they'd be more. He *wanted* more from her. But the reality of her life was starting to sink in.

Cici chatted with the staff and started looking through the racks of clothes. He had never been around babies. Maybe it was the nature of his upbringing but most of the homes he'd lived in up to and including the Fillions, with whom he'd lived from the age of ten, never had a lot of babies. They were the older kids that no one really wanted.

His Ma, that's what they all called Mrs. Fillion by her own design, had said that most couples didn't know what they were missing out on. Kids Hoop's age could walk, talk and take themselves to a bathroom; all plusses as far as she'd been concerned.

He was a big brother to lots of kids whose parents didn't have the time, but this was different. Already he was dreaming about Cici. Watching her as she listened to the shop girl tell her about the clothes she'd need for a newborn changed something inside of him, and he knew if he was going to pursue her he had to be honest.

With Cici of course, but also with himself.

If he wanted to be more than friends then he had to understand her life wasn't just her own. There was a baby. A child. No one knew better about how fragile life could be where they were concerned.

The fact that it was another man's baby didn't bother him. He didn't know his father and the love he had for his adoptive parents was a strong bond. And he considered Garrett a brother even though they weren't blood related. Hoop knew that blood wasn't the only bond that mattered.

The problem with Cici's pregnancy was that he didn't know … if he was ready to be a dad. If he could be in her life permanently … not that they were even *close* to that. But before he started something with her, he needed to really weigh up the consequences.

Dating her, he felt he sort of had to at least think about the long term. He didn't have to come to a hard answer at this moment but he knew that at some point it was going to be necessary.

"What do you think?" Cici asked him, holding a cute little t-shirt up to her belly. It was still flat, so to the outside eye it wouldn't be obvious she was pregnant.

"I like it," he said, realizing he was talking about more than

63

the clothing. He was talking about her and the pregnancy. He wanted a family of his own. Not that they were anywhere near being that type of couple, but there it was in the back of his mind. He wanted to be part of it from the beginning.

His palms started to sweat; he wiped them on his jeans and then his gaze met Cici's.

"Are you okay?"

He shrugged. "I need some air. I'm going to wait outside for you."

He didn't wait for her answer, just gave her a half smile and turned his back, exiting the shop.

It was hot outside and he pulled his sunglasses out before stepping out of the footpath to lean against the wall. He stared at the families and tourists all rushing past but didn't see them. Instead, his mind was still in the shop with Cici. If it were his kid, he'd be in there helping her choose but because they were "just friends" and because he wasn't sure what was going to happen between them, walking away had seemed like the right thing to do.

He was chasing his tail trying to be a good guy and trying to get what he wanted. But there was no easy answer. The easier thing would have been to just see where that damned kiss had lead back in February, when he'd been thinking with his mind instead of with his body and what had it gotten him?

He still might screw up with Cici even more than he already had. Still might make things awkward for his best friend and himself. Still might … need her more than he wanted to admit.

The door opened and he glanced up to see Cici standing there with a large bag in one hand and her sunglasses in the other.

"Finally catching up," she said.

"To what?"

"To where I am. It's hard to be friends when I have the baby and my future is going to be different," she said.

"It is. It's not the baby that's bothering me, Cici. It's me. I want to be your friend but I want you so damned much. Just being close to you makes my skin feel like it's too tight. And my gut is saying the only way to fix that is to spend a few hours in bed with you … but then what?"

"Well, I'm not sure. Do you think one night would be enough?" she asked.

"That's what's getting me. I have no idea and if we sleep together it will make things awkward in the future," he said. "I screwed up back in February."

"We both did," she said. "But let's spend the day together and see if we can at least be friends. *Real* friends and then we can figure out the rest of it."

New York harbor was busy with pleasure craft and ferries taking people to Ellis Island and the Statue of Liberty. But Cici was seated on the aft padded bench of a Chris-Craft Corsair hardtop. She didn't know that much about boats but Hoop was raving about it. He'd taken her on a tour of the cabin below deck, shown her the engine and told her that they'd be able to picnic on the bow of the boat when they anchored.

It was a pleasant weekend in June and the water was busy but there wasn't too much traffic to make it seem overwhelming.

She had been sitting by herself, staring out at the water and thinking too much. The shopping trip at Bonpoint had been fun until she'd stepped outside and been confronted with Hoop. Things were changing between them and would continue to do so unless she put a stop to it.

She liked him.

He was fun, sexy as hell and easy to get along with.

All winning qualities.

If she weren't pregnant she'd love to date him. See what happened between them and when it ended because she never could make anything last with a guy, she'd be happy to have the memories.

But she had the baby.

And then there was Hayley.

She and Garrett were planning a Valentine's Day wedding next year and she and Hoop would both be in the wedding party. And Cici was pretty sure that Garrett and Hayley were the real deal; that they'd spend the rest of their lives together, which meant if she slept with Hoop and ended things, Cici was probably going to lose Hayley too.

Not because Hayley would cut her out of her life, but because Cici would pull back.

And that was complicated. They weren't just friends, they were business partners. There was no point in her life that Hayley didn't touch.

"Water?" Hoop asked as he sat down at her feet.

She glanced over to find Alfonso and Lulu at the wheel of the boat.

"Yes, please," she said.

He handed her a bottle of water that was wet with condensation even from just a few minutes being out of the cooler.

That's how she felt around Hoop. Hot. *Too hot.* And she didn't know how to control it. She needed to figure it out.

"Ugh."

"What?"

"Just what you said earlier. We should definitely not keep hanging out together," she said. There. It was done. She'd said it out loud and now all she had to do was stick to it. Not back down.

"Agreed. But there's one problem," he said, lifting her legs up and scooting closer to her so that his thigh rested against the back of her thighs. He set her legs over his lap and took the water bottle from her. He took a long deep swallow and she watched his throat move as the water went down. He pushed his glasses up on his head and turned to stare at her with those blue-gray eyes of his.

"What's the problem?" she asked, but her mouth was dry and really she wasn't paying attention to his words. He'd taken his shirt off once they'd left the marina and his chest was tanned. His stomach flat and muscly but not like a photoshopped model's. He looked real and he felt solid next to her.

She wanted to reach out and touch him. To run her fingers over the light dusting of hair on his chest and follow it as it narrowed down into his waistband.

"I like you," he said. "There. I said it. I don't want to stop hanging out with you, Cici."

She swallowed against her dry throat. "But ..."

"Doesn't matter. Since February you have been on my mind. And since I finally cornered you two weeks ago at Shakespeare in the Park, I haven't stopped thinking about you. In fact, now that we've hung out, I know that you are as great as I thought you might be. I know that I want to keep hanging out with you. I know that I want to get to know you better."

"Then what was that panic attack at Bonpoint?" she asked. "You are conveniently forgetting about that."

"That was me ... not wanting to screw things up for your kid, but the truth is, for me at least, stopping seeing you isn't going to change the way I feel about it. It won't make me not like or care about you ..."

He trailed off and she knew it was her turn to pony-up with the honesty but she was scared. He'd been hurt. He'd had a long, lonely life and he'd carved out something for himself that made her proud of the man he was. He was being so honest and she knew she was going to have to at least meet him with the same honesty.

But she was scared.

Of Hoop?

Maybe.

Of the future?

Definitely.

Of taking another risk?

Yes.

That was the fear that kept her mouth closed. She didn't want to take a chance on him again. To him, it might have seemed like the music and their bodies brushing against each other at Olympus had brought them together but to her it had been raw attraction. A real spark of something and she'd asked him to take a chance on her and he'd said no.

So now he was asking her to do the same thing and she was afraid to say yes.

Because she knew she'd never been enough for any man.

Not her dad. Not her stepdad. Not any of the guys she'd dated. Not Rich.

Why would Hoop be different?

And if she weren't pregnant she'd say to hell with it and just go for it because she wanted Hoop. Really wanted him.

But she had the bean to think about and making dumb choices was in her past.

He put his hand on her thigh, his fingers lightly caressing her. Sensation spread from his fingers up her thigh and she shivered a little. The awareness of his nearness and his body that she'd been trying to ignore was impossible to overlook now.

Dammit.

Dumb choices weren't part of her past.

"Okay. Let's do it."

Chapter 7

Late afternoon bled into evening and Cici still wasn't sure what she'd agreed to. One thing was clear; Hoop seemed to have taken her agreement to mean that they were a couple.

He kept one arm around her as they sat next to each other on the bench enjoying the picnic that Alfonso had provided. It was delicious and though she might regret it tomorrow, she ate until she was stuffed.

"Why food?" Cici asked. "Hayley ... my partner at The Candied Apple & Café is drawn to desserts. She says that she can taste the combos just from smelling the ingredients."

Alfonso chuckled. "For me food has always meant family. I think the first time I met Hoop was at a cookout at his place. Everything important in my life has taken place while I was eating."

"You have cookouts?" she asked, turning to look at him.

He shrugged and she felt his arm tensing behind her. "Sometimes. A lot of the kids that I work with have busy working parents and sometimes don't get to experience that for themselves. I like to make sure that getting together is special."

"And food brings people together," Alfonso said. "That's how I won Lulu."

"He is a really good cook but he also looks good in his chef's whites," she said with a laugh.

"Do you cook, Cici?" Alfonso asked.

"Not at all. I can eat, but cooking? No, I don't have the patience for that. I hope someday to master some dish, something special that I can always fix for my baby," she said.

Alfonso looked at Hoop for a second and then back at her. "I can teach you a lot of easy dishes. Good comfort food and home cooking."

"I'd love that. I can … do you have someone who does your books?" she asked. She never liked to be in debt to someone. If Alfonso was going to teach her to cook she'd be more than happy to help him out in some way.

"Yeah. But I could use some help with my personal taxes," Alfonso replied.

"Don't do it, Cici. This guy's idea of bookkeeping is putting all of his receipts in a box under the bed. You'll be in there all day," Lulu said, smiling.

"I'm willing to give it a try if the cooking lessons are good. Also, I can set you up with some systems that will make it easier for the future."

"Deal," Alfonso said. "I can start whenever you want."

"I'll text you to set it up," Cici said.

"He's pretty good," Hoop said after they'd exchanged numbers.

"Can you cook?" she asked.

"He's pretty good in the kitchen if you like some sort of egg-based dish or meat on the grill," Alfonso said.

"I thought you said my chicken satay showed promise."

"Dude, I was being nice. Didn't want to diss your kitchen skills but the lady needs to know that you are a breakfast and grill cook."

Cici smiled to herself. Hoop seemed most of the time to have it all together. Nothing ever seemed to get in his way so it was nice to know he wasn't perfect at something.

"What are you smiling at?" he asked with a mock frown.

"Just thinking that you aren't perfect after all," she said.

"I'm not perfect at all," Hoop conceded.

"You just seem to have your stuff together," Cici said.

"He does," Lulu nodded. "When Alfonso first introduced us I was intimidated."

Hoop looked over at Lulu. "You know I think you're ideal for Alfonso. Nothing to be intimidated about. I always sing your praises. You tamed this crazy man."

"It was an uphill battle," Lulu said.

"I didn't think I was that bad," Alfonso jumped in.

"He thought that a month was a long-term relationship," Lulu said to Cici.

Cici could see that Alfonso and Lulu were content and that Hoop was very much a part of their … well, family, for lack of a better word. But Lulu and Hoop were ganging up on Alfonso so Cici decided to take his side.

"That might have more to do with the quality of singletons on the market than Alfonso," Cici said.

"Perhaps. I was in a prior relationship when he was in his long-term thing," Lulu said.

Alfonso reached over and scooped Lulu off the bench and onto his lap. He brought his mouth down on hers in a passion-filled kiss and when he lifted his head, both of them looked flushed.

"All of that changed when we met. It makes a difference when you find the one," Alfonso said.

The one.

"Do you think there is really one for each of us?" Hoop asked, once Lulu and Alfonso went out on the deck.

She looked over at Hoop. She'd dated a lot. Many of them clearly not the one. "I have no idea. To be honest, I've never been looking for one."

"You haven't?"

71

"Have you? I mean life is busy with getting the Candied Apple & Café going and it's hard when a relationship takes a lot of energy and it seems like keeping things light is just … well, easier," Cici said.

More than once she'd thought about maybe getting serious but then when she'd met Hoop it was different. "When we met that night at the club, I thought you were a great guy. The kind of man I wanted to get serious with. But then …"

She stopped. She didn't really want to reveal the big ugly mess she was inside. How she almost didn't feel like she was good enough for a guy who had his shit together like Hoop. Most of her life she'd been running from mistakes. But admitting it to a man whose only flaw so far was that he could only cook breakfast food or grill meat? Well, she wasn't going to do that.

"I screwed up," Hoop said. "I'm not flawless, Cici. I make all kinds of mistakes. I have a great family and I know I should be grateful for them and I am. But then another part of me always wonders why I have to be thankful for what everyone else seems to just take for granted."

She sat back staring at him. His words resonated deep inside of her. In that spot where she sometimes resented Steve because he loved the boys more than her. But he had never treated her poorly, she just wanted more. And here was Hoop who'd had nothing.

"That's only natural," she said.

He shrugged. "I don't know. I mean everyone says I'm lucky to have ended up at the Fillions' and I know I am, but damn, once in a while it would have been nice to complain about how mom is always trying to set me up, but someone always points out that she's the mom she didn't have to be," Hoop said.

Cici finally heard the pain in Hoop's voice. She scooted closer, put her arms around him and hugged him tightly to her. "Being an adult is hard."

He laughed and pulled her closer. "There is one thing about it that I like."

"What's that?" she asked.

"This," he said, lowering his mouth and kissing her.

He tasted like sunshine and sea and she closed her eyes and had a flashback to Jamaica. The smell of the salty ocean had been in the air that night. But she'd been drunk on champagne and searching for something to make her feel better about herself.

In retrospect, Rich's kisses were sloppy.

Hoop was nothing like that. He tasted right to her. She opened her mouth a little wider and coaxed her tongue into his mouth, trying to taste more of him. He groaned and pulled her closer. She wrapped her arms around him and held him for what felt like forever before she pulled back, looking up at him. His lips were swollen and his skin flushed.

He didn't say anything and she was glad of it. She was afraid if he tried to talk to her now she'd start rambling and say something she regretted.

Hoop hadn't meant to get all heavy about his past but there were times when he heard himself described as perfect or flawless, like today, which made him feel at his limits. There was no way he could be less than Mom had raised him to be. He *had* to be a good guy. He knew how to cook eggs because she'd taught him and Pops had taught him to grill.

But they had a lot of rules and hadn't been forgiving of mistakes. Mom had been the one to tell him that most of the people he met would be waiting for him to fail because of how he'd come into the world. That he had to remember that. And he did. He worked with Big Brothers and met guys like Alfonso who never had anyone to tell them that.

To say that just because society expects someone from a certain background to be a punk doesn't mean that was the only option.

Cici turned him on. She made him want to be a better man, but he knew that he wanted to be more than that to her. He didn't want to be the good friend. The guy she could safely date.

Because there wasn't one damned safe thing about how he felt about her.

He wanted to know everything about her. Wanted to dig deeply and find all of her "flaws" and show her his. He didn't want to find a perfect relationship with her because that wasn't real. He'd heard the Fillions fighting often enough to know that love wasn't quiet romance all the time.

He wanted that.

But he also didn't want to turn into someone who could potentially push her away.

So, he was playing the good guy. Never admitting that he was jealous of Rich Maguire, some two-bit actor who knocked Cici up and then turned his back on her. Angry. Damn, but he was good and angry at himself and a little bit at Cici.

But he wasn't going to say any of that. Not to her.

Not now.

And probably not ever.

"You are a good kisser," she said at last.

He shouldn't have kissed her, he thought. Yet it was what he wanted. But he could tell she hadn't been prepared for it. "So are you."

"Tell me something that's not perfect about you," she said as they sat on the edge of his yacht in the marina. Alfonso and Lulu had gone back to their place and he'd asked her if she wanted to stay. They were sitting on deck chairs facing the skyline. He had thought how lucky he was to live in this city. The views were perfect.

He was a lucky guy.

He knew it but it was easier sometimes to pretend that life wasn't as easy as it sometimes seemed for him. He'd been the youngest boy in the Fillion home while he'd been growing up. They hadn't adopted any more kids after him.

His siblings all said he was spoiled because he was the baby. And to some extent that was true. He had been taken care of by the Fillions and treated really well. Part of it was that he was

74

older when he got to them and they tried to make up for years of him being adrift.

"Do you really have to think that hard to come up with something that you aren't good at?"

He shook his head. "I wasn't very good at being a cop."

"Yeah?"

He nodded and she watched him a lot like she wasn't sure how to take him. He realized that was because of Garrett. She wasn't simply a woman he'd asked out; she'd seen him with his guard down with his boys on a poker night.

"Why not? Seems like you are the kind of guy who likes to be the best."

"I do. But … this is not going to do anything for my argument but I hated to see perps who were making choices because they thought they were owed something."

"I bet," she said. "I mean if anyone were owed something it would be you."

"No. No one is owed anything. We have to find our path, work and make our way. I mean that's it. I wasn't very sympathetic and some of my collars were really in a tough spot and had made the best decision they could."

The breeze blew, bringing the smell of the sea and the hibachi grill someone was using to cook stir-fry. She tucked that long strand of hair that was always blowing around her face behind her ear. "Good thing you were smart enough to change careers."

"Good thing," Hoop said. Now he had a chance to become a partner … he didn't regret his choice; it felt like validation.

"How did you choose law?"

"Pops is a lawyer and when I was home one weekend talking about changing careers he suggested I take a leave of absence and do some internships. The first one was at his practice. I found I really liked it. I could make a difference to the people who needed it. Family law is difficult. It's hard for people who feel like they have no options to make the right choice."

"Like me," she said.

"Do you feel trapped?"

She shrugged and nibbled on her lower lip as she toyed with the charm on her necklace. She stared at the Manhattan skyline and didn't say anything. He wondered if she was going to answer when she dropped the charm and looked over at him. There was seriousness in her eyes that hadn't been there before.

"No. It's odd because being a mom has never been in my plans but once I found out about the bean," she patted her stomach, "I just started changing. Like maybe this was my reason to grow up, you know?"

He didn't know. Not really. But he could see what the baby had done to her. He hadn't really known her before her pregnancy but he liked the woman she was now.

"I do," he said.

Cici knew it was time for her to go but she didn't want to leave. She wanted to stay with Hoop and see if the kisses and the touches were going to live up to their billing. She suspected they would. But part of her wanted to stay because of the sun and the day they'd spent together. Another part ... well, to see how he'd react after.

Was he sincere when he said he wanted to be friends and would stay by her side or was that just a line?

Chances were it was legit. She was learning that Hoop was a man of his word. But neither of them knew what this parenthood thing was going to be like. And she was just starting to sort out the paternity agreement she wanted Rich to sign. And Hoop was going for junior partner, something that would demand a lot of his time.

Starting anything right now wasn't the best idea.

Given everything that he'd revealed to her today, she suspected he wasn't playing her. But she'd been wrong before and she really, well to be honest, she really liked Hoop. She realized how shallow her affection had been when she'd gone to Jamaica. She would never have suspected half of what Hoop really was.

"Why are you looking at me like that?" he asked, as he came back on deck bringing them some fresh drinks. He was drinking something that looked like whiskey neat and she was downing water like she had just run a marathon. Trying to pretend that she didn't miss alcohol.

Dang. She'd hoped he'd just sort of sweep her up in his arms so she wouldn't have to think. But she was already dwelling too much on what could happen.

She hadn't realized how often she leaned on alcohol to ease the decision-making process. She needed to figure this out for herself. Champagne had been responsible for her getting into this situation and it looked like bottled water and her own judgment were going to be in charge this time.

"Trying to decide if I should go home or stay here with you." Once the words were out she didn't regret them. In fact, as she watched him leaning back next to her, everything she wanted out of this evening coalesced.

Hoop had changed into a pair of shorts when they'd gotten on the boat which showed off his long, tanned legs. He had his sunglasses pushed up on the top of his head and he stood there, his head tipped to the side smiling at her.

There was something mischievous in his smile and the way he watched her gave her shivers. The good kind. The kind that she'd experienced the first time he kissed her.

And she knew all the reasons why she should just turn around and leave his boat, but none of them mattered.

Even the mental pro/con list she had going wasn't going to change her mind.

Her gut said Hoop was who she needed to be with. Tonight.

"How's it going?" he asked in that droll way he had when he was trying to be nonchalant.

"It's harder than you might think," she said.

He threw his head back and laughed. "Nah, I know how hard it is."

She shook her head. "Stop it. You just make me want to straddle you and find out."

"Come on, Cici," he said putting his glass on the deck and holding out his hand.

It was a big strong hand. She stopped thinking. Why was she trying to analyze this? She'd never been good at it. He wasn't like a number on a spreadsheet. No matter how many times she tried to force the columns to balance. It wasn't going to happen. Not yet.

Not until she had all the information.

Pretending she didn't want him. Learning more than she'd expected to about him. Everything swirled around as she put her water on the deck and stood up. Glamorous as ever, she tripped over her flip-flop and sort of fell on him instead of the sexy way she'd planned to straddle him.

He grunted as he caught her and she started laughing. Of course, when she wanted to be graceful she wasn't. It wasn't like she was always klutzy. This was … she didn't know what. If she had to guess she'd say it was nerves.

He joined her with a shout of laughter a second later.

"If there is anything that sums us up it is this moment," he said.

"What?"

"Not perfect," he said. "I think that means we are real."

"You think so?"

"Yes. I always try to be what a woman wants but with you I keep faltering on the starting block. Not one time have I done what's necessary to get you into my arms. But you are here now and that's … well that's enough."

"For me too."

Chapter 8

Hoop held Cici closer to him than he wanted to. He wanted to be blasé. To pretend she hadn't just made a place for herself deep inside his soul but that was a lie. Sweet, awkward and totally adorable, she was drawing him under her spell without even trying.

She was a soft weight on his chest and she looked up at him with those deep chocolate brown eyes of hers, and he saw the nerves and the excitement. He lifted his hands and framed her face, pushed her hair back and thought how much his life was changing without her seeming to be aware of it.

She licked her lips; they were soft and pink and he knew how good she tasted when he kissed her. He hardened as she squirmed around on his lap trying to get comfortable.

"I guess falling on you didn't dampen the mood," she said with a nervous giggle. It was so unlike Cici that he smiled back at her.

"Nothing would dampen it now," he said. "I've been watching you all day, wanting you. Hoping I didn't screw things up by saying something … stupid."

"You aren't a stupid man, Hoop," she said, putting her hands on his shoulders as she straddled his thighs. She sat back and looked at him. "I don't want you to regret …"

He put his fingers over her lips. "No. Don't say it. We've been trying to do the sensible thing since we met and you know what?"

She shook her head.

"We're still dancing around each other, wanting each other more and more. Or at least I am."

"I am too," she said. "You're right. It kind of seems silly to keep waiting and trying not to."

"I know. I'm right a lot," he said smiling.

"You're so not," she said. "You just spent a good portion of the afternoon telling me all of your flaws."

"Damn. I did, didn't I?"

"Yup. So now I know you're not perfect," she said, absently caressing the side of his neck.

Until that moment he'd had no idea that he could be so turned on by such a gentle caress. But her finger idling moving over the column of his neck was having a direct impact on his erection. It was as if she were stroking him there as well.

"Perfect is overrated," he said, his voice slightly huskier than he'd have liked. But the woman had an effect on him and he wasn't ashamed to let her know it.

"Exactly. I'm flawed," she said. "Before you see me naked you should know I have a poochy stomach. I don't look like a model."

"I don't have a six pack," he said. "Does that make you want me any less?"

"Not at all. I want you because of the way your kisses make me feel and how you taste better than almost anything I've tried before and that includes chocolate."

"Then why would you think I'd expect you to look like a model?" he asked. Her words made his blood flow heavier and he knew that he wanted her more than he had ever desired any other woman.

She shrugged. "Men are different."

"Boys are shallow that way," Hoop said. "Men aren't. Wrap your legs around my waist."

"Why?" she asked, but she scooted closer, rubbing her center over his groin and he groaned.

"I'm going to carry you downstairs and make love to you."

"Oh," she said.

Just oh. She rested her head against his chest and wrapped her arms around his shoulders and her legs around his waist. He stood up carefully and held her with both arms as he walked down the galley way to the large queen-sized bunk in the bow of the yacht. The bunk took up the entire length of the room and had only a narrow path at the end. He lifted her and set her on the end of the bunk and then stepped back.

She put her hands behind her and leaned back on them, looking up at him. The skirt from her sundress was high on her thighs and he noticed she had really nice legs. Actually, he'd noticed that before. The night they'd gone dancing at Olympus she'd had on a really short skirt.

"You have nice legs."

She arched one eyebrow at him. "Thank you."

Lame, Hooper. Lame.

He wanted to bring his A game to the bedroom with her. But she rattled him. Every-damn-thing about Cici rattled him.

He kicked off his boat shoes and climbed onto the bed next to her. She turned to face him as he was leaning in and their foreheads bumped and then she laughed. That nervous-excited sound she'd made earlier. He put his hand on her jaw, stroked her lips with his thumb.

"Why are we so awkward?" she asked.

He shrugged. He definitely wasn't going to tell her that he wanted this so badly that he was afraid of making a mistake. Of coming too quickly. And there was a very real chance of that because just sitting on the bed with her had him hard. And she smelled good and the way she'd placed her hand on his thigh, her fingers falling between his legs, was doing nothing to help his control.

"We both must really want this," he said at last.

"I do. I can't stop thinking about you," she said, using her free hand to push up the hem of his shirt. Her fingers against his side were cold as she squeezed against him. Then she opened her fingers and caressed her way up his chest, bringing the fabric of his t-shirt with her.

He reached down and tore it up and over his head, tossing it aside. He glanced down at his chest. He wasn't flabby but he wasn't ripped either. He worked out when he had the time and between his work hours and his obsession with seeing Cici as often as he could, he really hadn't made the time for the gym.

She glanced up at him.

"What?"

"You're not breathing," she said.

"Just wishing I'd worked out more in the last few weeks," he said.

She used her hand in the middle of his chest to push him back and he let her. Falling back and bracing himself on his arms. She straddled him again and this time she put both hands on his shoulders.

"Stop it. We are both normal people. We're not Hollywood hotties. We're real," she said.

She brushed her lips over his and he parted his underneath hers and her tongue slipped inside. He lifted one hand and held the back of her head as the kiss deepened. He was addicted to her and as the kiss continued his mind pretty much shut off as his body took over. He'd been waiting way too long to have her in his arms.

He pushed his hands up underneath the skirt of her dress, her thighs were firm and smooth but he kept moving his hands upward until he could cup her buttocks and draw her more fully over him. He pushed his hands under the soft fabric of her underwear, tracing his finger along her smooth skin.

She arched her back and pulled her mouth from his. Her skin

was flushed light pink and her pupils dilated. She reached down and tugged her sundress up and over her head. As she lifted her arms, her breasts were bared to him. She had on a small bandeau style bra and he brought one hand to the bra, pulling it up and over her head. She put her hands on her waist and looked down at him, but her breasts transfixed him. They were full and had pink nipples that puckered as he stared at them. He reached up and ran his finger around the edge of each one until they tightened even more.

With a groan he shifted forward until he could take her in his mouth. He suckled her, pulling the nipple deep into his mouth. He felt her hands on his shoulders kneading his skin and her hips rocked back and forth over him.

He urged her to continue, riding his erection with his hand on her hip. He was painfully hard now, his shorts constricting him and he reached between them to lower his zipper but her hands were already there.

She undid the snap on his shorts and then lowered the zipper and reached into the opening to stroke him through the fabric of his boxer briefs. He pulled his mouth from her breast and lifted her off his lap, long enough to finish getting undressed. He glanced over at Cici to see she'd taken her underwear off as well and now knelt next to him completely bare.

He caught his breath as he stared at her. Her skin was lightly tanned except for her stomach which was white and she did have the tiniest little bump of stomach. His gaze skimmed lower, noticing that the hair between her legs was light brown and neatly trimmed.

He reached out to touch her. To follow the path he'd just taken with his gaze. He skimmed the tan lines on her shoulders and the vee that plunged between her breasts from the sun she'd gotten earlier today. He drew his finger around the full globes of her breasts and her nipples darkened as he touched her. He leaned forward to drop nibbling kisses along the same path. Following his fingers down the center of her body to her belly button where he teased her with his tongue before letting his hand drift lower.

Her thighs parted and he lifted his head to look at her, reached between her parted thighs to touch her most feminine flesh. She was damp and he lightly caressed her before drawing his hand back to her thighs. He caressed his way down one leg to her knee and then back up. This time he parted her center and lightly tapped on her clitoris with his finger.

She moaned and parted her thighs further as she took him in her hand. She stroked his length and his hips jutted forward in her grip. She felt so good. He closed his eyes, grasping for a little self-discipline so he could make this last, but instead he was assailed by the scent of her. The fresh springy scent of her hair, the musk of her womanhood and mingling scent of sea and skin.

He opened his eyes, moving forward to push her gently onto her back. She lay down and he kept one hand between her legs, lightly caressing her while he suckled at her breast. His erection was nestled next to her thigh and he arched his hips, rubbing himself against her as he caressed her.

Her hips rocked on the bed and her legs scissored back and forth against him as he drove her higher and higher. She made soft little sounds in the back of her throat and he could feel the urgency in her movements as she got closer and closer to the edge. Her hand grasped him.

He jerked his hips back, away from her touch, lifting his head from her breast and watching her as she arched under his touch and then she cried out his name. He leaned over her, thrusting his tongue deep into her mouth and she sucked it even deeper. Her hands clinging to his shoulders as she rode his fingers, thrusting against him again and again until she shuddered in his arms and tore her mouth from his.

She looked up at him into his eyes and he saw an emotion there that made him feel too much. He wanted this to be more physical but he couldn't forget he was here with Cici. He framed her face with his hands again, pushing her bangs from her face and leaning down, resting his forehead against hers. The tip of his manhood nudged her opening.

He shifted his hips back but hesitated. Looked down into those wide brown eyes of hers and knew after this moment everything would change between them.

He wasn't going to be able to go back to pretending she was just a pretty girl he wanted to have sex with. Or a friend of a friend that he was attracted to. After this moment he'd know what it was like to feel her wrapped around him and he knew that he'd never be able to forget it.

He pushed forward, entering her and he wanted to plunge all the way home but instead he took his time. Forced himself to go slowly, entering her inch-by-inch until he was fully seated.

She moaned a little and he looked down to see her eyes were closed and she had the softest smile on her face. She wrapped her legs around his hips and locked her heels at the small of his back, pushing him into her as she arched underneath him.

He drew his hips back and meant to keep the pace slow, to let it build but she did that thing with her heels again and he found himself driving into her. He pushed one hand underneath her body, gripping her backside and holding her to him while he pounded into her.

Her hips answered, meeting each plunge of his and he felt a tingle run down his spine but he didn't want to come until she did. Wanted to feel her pulsing around him. He reached between their bodies and rubbed her clitoris. Her nails dug into his back and he heard that long, low moan from her as she tightened around him. He couldn't help driving himself into her again and again and then his hips jerked as he jetted his release into her. He kept thrusting until he was empty and then collapsed on her gently, fully spent.

He rested his head on her shoulder and she held him to her, her hands running up and down his back. He closed his eyes, wanted to make this moment last. This moment when he didn't have to think about anything except holding Cici. But his mind was already running through the options. Could he ask her to spend the night with him? Should he?

What if he did and she said no?

Why did he want to make love to her again? Once wasn't enough.

He needed to stake his claim. To make her his. Claim her as he wished he'd done months ago at Olympus.

And she was carrying another man's baby. He knew that shouldn't bother him. Rationally it didn't. But on some primal level he wanted to claim the baby as his as well.

He was in a dangerous spot.

He hadn't felt like this ever before.

"Hoop?"

"Hmm …"

"Thank you," she said.

He lifted his head and looked down at her.

"Why are you thanking me?"

"That was pretty spectacular."

"It was for me too," he admitted. She'd scooted up on the bed and rested on the pillows. He pulled her into his arms.

She cuddled close to him, wrapping her arm around his chest and draping one leg over his thighs. She yawned.

He held her to him. "I think we are definitely more than friends now."

"We are. This doesn't feel complicated," she said in a sleepy voice.

He just held her to him as she drifted off to sleep. But a part of him realized that this didn't feel complicated for her because she was exhausted from the sex, the sun and their first day together. He suspected when she woke she'd be assaulted with the same worries he was.

He liked her. A lot. He wasn't sure if knew what love was or if he'd feel that way about Cici at some point, but right now he just wanted to keep her in his arms and safe.

He wanted to let the world know she was his. And that possessiveness worried him. He had never been possessive about anyone or truly anything. He'd known from his earliest memory that life was transient. Things and people moved in and out of his life.

But he wanted to keep her.

He knew she wasn't an object but there was something deep inside of him that wanted to just hold on and never let her go.

But he knew that would freak her out.

Hell, he was freaked and it was his own thoughts that were doing it.

He had to give her space. Give himself space.

He needed to be normal. He had to figure out how to pretend that sex had been great but not life-altering. Because he had no idea if it had been life altering for her.

And really, how did a guy ask a girl that?

She'd said the sex was great.

That was a step in the right direction.

The sounds of the harbor as it settled down for the night lulled him to a contented sleep. He kept Cici cuddled close to him throughout the night but when he woke he found he was alone in the bed.

The steely light of dawn filled the room and as he glanced around the small bunk he could find no trace of her. Her clothes were gone and he listened to see if she was still on the boat but he heard nothing. He got up, pulled on his shorts and ran up to the deck to make sure he was alone.

And he was. His heart was racing and he felt a little bit angry that she'd left like she had.

Without a note or a word or anything.

Chapter 9

Cici got as far as the main office of the marina before she had second thoughts about just leaving.

Running away.

Again.

That was her way of dealing with problems she didn't want to face. And it had been for longer than she wanted to admit. She pulled her sunglasses from her large bag and put them on and then looked around for a bench. Right there in direct view of Hoop's yacht.

Instead she decided to keep walking. She'd told herself she was going home but the more she walked the less she wanted to be alone. She stopped at a coffee shop and ordered a herbal tea for herself and a coffee for Hoop. She also picked out an assortment of pastries and then determinedly walked back to the marina.

Last night was the first time in a long time that she'd had sex with a man and she hadn't been drinking. There hadn't been the inhibition freeing power of alcohol to convince her she was making the right decision or make her not care if she wasn't. She'd chosen to sleep with Hoop.

And that was why she'd left.

She hadn't slept so peacefully in a long time. It was easy to say that it was him, but a part of her knew she had simply been exhausted. From the pregnancy and the day in the sun, but also from resisting Hoop for as long as she had.

It had taken more energy than she'd expected it to.

And he had been a very thorough lover. She still tingled when she thought about being back in that bed with him.

She took her time, her steps slowing as she got back to his yacht.

The Lazy Sunday.

That was the name of his boat. She wondered if it meant something or if it were already named when he purchased it.

She knew she was delaying, but now that she was back, she worried he might have woken and knew she'd already cleared out.

"You're back."

Well, hell. Of course, he had woken. Nothing was easy where they were concerned.

"I am."

She pushed her sunglasses to the top of her head with the hand holding the pastries and tipped her head back to look over at him.

He wore only his shorts, which hung low on his hips and had his arms crossed over his naked chest. His eyes were hard to read from this distance but his body language was defensive.

It hit her that she wasn't the only one who could be hurt. That despite the fact that they had joked yesterday that he only had a few flaws, Hoop was vulnerable to her just as she was to him.

"Can I come back on board?" she asked.

"Yes," he said.

She climbed up the gangplank very carefully. She hadn't been clumsy at all when she'd walked to the marina but simply being close to Hoop made her feel like she might miss a step or slip.

Something she didn't want to do. Not now.

He reached for the cardboard holder that held the hot drinks and as soon as she was within arm's reach she handed them to him.

"Want to eat up here or down in the galley?" he asked.

"Down, I think" she replied. The harbor was starting to get busy and she felt … raw. She knew there was no way she could just be blasé about last night or about Hoop.

And she was still a mess. It didn't matter that she'd already decided that being herself was the only way to move forward. She was trying that. But she hadn't counted on the fact that every time she was just Cici she made mistakes and missteps and had to deal with the consequences.

And that was what was bothering her this morning. Last night hadn't felt like a mistake.

But she wanted something more for Hoop than she could give him. The man who'd grown up as he had, even though he'd turned out wonderful, deserved a wife and a family of his own. She wagered that he'd be a very dedicated family man when the time came and in her mind, as wrong as it may be, she wanted him to have a family that was his.

She followed him down the steps into the galley and he slid onto the curved bench behind the table, taking a seat opposite him. She put the bag of pastries in front of her and tore the paper so that he could see what was inside.

Acid swirled in her stomach, not nerves but morning sickness. She might have left eating too late.

She reached for a buttery croissant, tore a bite off and just as she brought it to her mouth, she felt her stomach heave. She dropped the pastry and ran for the head. Swallowing and trying to keep the morning sickness at bay.

She got sick. It was worse today than it had been in a week. But she put that down to her emotional state.

She felt a wet washcloth against the back of her neck and when she stood up, Hoop handed her a glass of water. She rinsed her mouth with it and spit it into the sink before flushing.

She looked up in the mirror over the sink and saw him standing there, watching her. He didn't hide the emotion on his face, but that didn't mean she had a clue what it meant. It looked like he cared and maybe was a little worried for her.

"Sorry," she said. "I have to eat first thing or else."

"It's okay," he said. "Can you eat now?"

"Not for a little while," she said. "But I think I'm ready for my tea."

He squeezed her shoulder and then turned and walked back to the table. She didn't understand how but something had changed between them. As she sat there sipping her tea, listening to Hoop make light conversation about the harbor, she realized it was that the anger and fear had left them. Throwing up had burned through the inhibitions they both had this morning.

Interesting.

He'd been mad when he'd woken up alone, no doubt about that. But she'd come back. She'd come back and brought coffee and then she'd reminded him that she was pregnant and dealing with a lot of emotional and physical stuff that she wasn't used to.

It had been the wake-up call he'd needed to remind himself that he and Cici were in unchartered territory here. Sex had been great, as he'd long suspected it would be, but it was past time for them to just be lovers.

He cared about her. More deeply than he had anyone else. He wanted to protect her, make her happy. Make her his. But that was something deep in his DNA that he couldn't change.

He was a modern guy, he got that she was her own woman and that she really couldn't belong to him, but all the same some primal part of him wanted to claim her.

She watched him with amusement in her eyes and that made him feel like he was ten feet tall. He'd done that. Well, him and morning sickness.

Who'd have thought the act of throwing up would be a tension breaker?

"What?"

"Nothing. I just love how much you love the city."

He shrugged. "It's been the one constant in my life. No matter where I ended up in foster homes, whatever the situation was, I could always come here to the harbor and watch the boats. Water … it soothes me."

"Are you a Pisces?"

"What does that have to do with anything?"

"My little brothers are both Pisces and my mom used to put them in the bath tub when they were little and getting ornery. Always just calmed them down."

"I am Pisces," he admitted, surprised. "I never thought about water and my astrological sign before."

"First time for everything," she said, taking a small bite of the croissant.

He watched her as she chewed carefully and then swallowed. He was ready to spring into action if she couldn't keep the bite down. She gave him a little half smile.

"All good," she said. "Thank God. I don't think my dignity could handle throwing up in front of you one more time."

"It wasn't that bad," he said.

"Maybe from your side," she said, with a wink. "Seriously, I'm sorry."

"It's okay, Cici. Morning sickness is just part of the process," he said.

"Not about getting sick. For bugging out like I did," she said.

He leaned back against the padded seat back. "Why did you?"

He had eaten a bear claw—a pastry that was filled with almond paste—and finished his coffee. She'd bought a large cinnamon roll and an éclair as well and he was tempted to eat something else but she was pregnant and he remembered his sister said she had been hungry. A lot. So Hoop waited.

93

"Everything seemed different this morning and I wasn't sure if you would want me to stay or if I wanted to stay. I got really nervous and just decided to leave," she admitted.

"I missed you when I woke up," he said gently. "I'm glad you came back."

He wasn't sure what it was about Cici but she made him say things that normally he would keep to himself. But with her he didn't want to. He wanted her to know how deeply she affected him.

"Me too," she said. "Are you done eating?"

"I was waiting for you. My brother-in-law warned me to never get between an expectant mother and food."

Cici laughed as he'd hoped she would. "Well, I can only eat one of these."

She picked up the éclair and he took the cinnamon roll and started eating it.

"I'm curious about your family," she said. "My stepdad was always very careful to draw a line between me and my half-brothers. I never really felt like his daughter … but your family wasn't like that, was it?"

"Not at all. We were all the same," Hoop said. "Tommy, my oldest brother is Mom and Pops' biological son but they never treated any of us as if we were different. I didn't come to them until I older so I was used to being an outsider, but my mom wouldn't let me be. She treated me like I was hers from the first moment we met."

Cici nodded. "She sounds like a really good woman."

"She is. I'd love for you to meet her and my Pops too. They'd like you."

"You think so?" she asked. "I'm not sure I'm ready to meet your folks, Hoop."

"I know. But start thinking about it. We have a big Fourth of July party at their place in Montauk. I want you to come with me."

He hadn't meant to invite her. She'd just left him while he was sleeping. He wasn't sure that he trusted her. It was only June. But he was grasping at any reason to keep her close.

But she'd come back.

He wanted that to be significant. He really felt like there was something between the two of them. His folks were the best litmus test he had for seeing if something was real. They'd helped with college, careers and even past relationships. And with Cici he felt like she was different and a part of him wanted their feedback to make sure he wasn't fooling himself because of sex.

"I'll think about it. My mom and stepdad have a summer cottage in Sag Harbor. If we go to your folks for the Fourth I'm going to have to tell my mom I'm pregnant and visit her as well."

What?

"You haven't told her yet?" Hoop asked.

"Nope. Well to be fair I haven't known all that long," she said. "It's just if I tell her, she's going to ask about the father and if he's in the picture and I wasn't ready for that conversation before. But I think I am now," she admitted.

He hoped so.

He hadn't realized how *much* she was running from until that moment. She'd said she needed time and as usual he'd ignored it and just pushed ahead for what he wanted. He hoped that he hadn't made a mistake in doing so.

Telling Hoop that she hadn't mentioned to her parents that she was pregnant really drove home the fact that she hadn't been ready to face up to anything yet. She'd been in denial for a long time. Hadn't wanted to face anything to do with the baby or Rich until she'd moved. Then she'd decided to start carving out her own path.

But there were still parts of it that had to be dealt with. Things that she wouldn't be able to leave behind as easily as a sublet house. He'd sort of thought that time was standing still until she had finished processing everything but it wasn't. She was nearing the end of the first trimester and really she needed to talk to her mom about being pregnant.

Though her parents were back from their vacation with her brothers, she'd resisted going home for a visit. She wasn't sure what she was going to say but she knew she should call them.

She'd do it. But not right now. Now she was going to just enjoy this lazy morning with Hoop. Pretend that she had few worries.

"I'm not judging," Hoop said. "Honestly, there are times when the last people I want to talk to are my folks so I get it. But I think this is one of those things that will only get harder with time."

She rubbed the back of her neck. She knew that. Did he think she didn't know that? But when she glanced up she saw just that same kindness on his face that made her feel like a big meanie.

"Ugh. I thought I should sort out stuff with Rich first. I had no idea what his response would be and he's one of my cousin's husband's best friends. So it's bound to come up at some point."

"On that subject. I heard you met with Lilia. How'd that go?" he asked. "Do you think she'll work for you?"

"Yes. I liked her a lot. She sent over the draft of the paperwork and I reviewed it, but honestly I have no idea what I'm supposed to look for," she admitted. The paper was like a contract except that it dealt with the baby and herself and personal things instead of business arrangements. It had been weird to read and she'd truly had no idea what to do with it next.

"I'm sure it's all in order. The legalese protects the both of you. Do you want me to go over it with you?" he asked.

Did she? "Lilia explained it all to me. I asked her to add in something so that our child can contact him and his family one day. I don't know if the baby is going to want to know him or not. What do you think?"

"If it were me, I'd want to know. Hell, I tried to find out who my dad and mom were when I was an adult. It's just a big empty hole inside of me at times," Hoop admitted.

He leaned forward as he spoke and she could see why he was good at his job. There was a real note of sincerity in his voice; and confidence. Her heart ached. For him and for her little bean. It was hard to think that her decisions now were going to affect the child as an adult.

"Thank you for sharing that," she said. "I want to make sure I'm doing the right thing but also I want to respect Rich's wishes."

"Would you get together with him if he said he thought that was best for the child?" Hoop asked tentatively.

"I don't think so. I mean, we hardly know each other and this entire situation hasn't put him in the best light," she said, looking over at Hoop as something else nudged at her subconscious.

The fact that Rich wasn't Hoop. He wasn't sitting here quietly with her talking about things that were complicated. He hadn't seen her get sick from the pregnancy and he hadn't made love to her the way Hoop had.

"I want this to work," she said at last. Hoop was important to her. She couldn't guess if he would continue to be in the coming months as her pregnancy continued but for right now he was.

"Me too," Hoop said.

Her phone pinged and she glanced at her watch first before digging her phone out of her bag. It was after nine.

"I'm late for brunch with Hayley and Iona," Cici said.

"I didn't realize you had plans for today," Hoop said.

"We have a standing date for mimosas and egg white omelets," Cici said. "Though I've been having orange juice instead of mimosas."

She pulled her phone from her bag and verified the text was from Iona.

Iona: *You okay? We are at the Plaza.*

Cici: *I'm good. Hanging with Hoop this morning.*

Iona: *Want details. Be prepared to spill tomorrow. Xoxo*

Cici smiled to herself. She understood how someone who wasn't related by blood could be closer than family. She felt that way about Hayley and Iona, but the parent child bond, that one still worried her. Was she doing a disservice to Hoop by starting something with him and knowing that he might never really have a solid relationship with her child or would he, because of his own upbringing, be able to love her child as if it were his own?

And when was she going to relax enough to take a chance on that happening.

"I'm free for the rest of the day," she said. "Do you want to spend it with me?"

He nodded. "I'd like that. A lot. What did you have in mind?"

Chapter 10

Cici looked a bit like a deer in the headlights when he said he'd spend the afternoon with her. And really, who could blame her. She'd been trying to make her escape already once today and while he appreciated that she'd come back and offered to spend the day with him, a part of him wanted to let her off the hook and say he had work to do.

The truth was he did have work to do.

But with Cici, he'd gone against his instincts once and stepped back and look what had happened. She'd hooked up with another guy and was having his baby … he couldn't help the twinge of pain that thought induced. All his life he'd wanted things: relationships, jobs, opportunities, but always in the back of his mind was the thought that maybe he wasn't good enough. That maybe he didn't deserve them.

And he wanted to be good enough.

Hell, he knew he was. He was a decent man. He had a great job, a good family and no matter what that aching feeling of emptiness in his soul sometimes whispered to him, he had a good life.

"I've got two thoughts for the afternoon," he said, as they stood on the deck of his yacht.

"Two?"

"Yes," he said. "We take the yacht out again and sail around."

"Or?" she asked.

"We go into the city. I will be happy to paddle you around the lake in Central Park or we can go to the Highline and pretend to be tourists."

"Tourists? When have you ever done that?" she asked with a smile in her voice but he could tell that it was a little strained around the edges.

"Garrett and I used to do it when we were teenagers. We'd go to Times Square and gawk at the signs and ask people to take our photo. When they'd ask where we were from we'd say Queens … it was priceless to see the expression on their faces."

She shook her head. He had told her they would be friends no matter what. "That's insane. I can't picture you doing something like that."

He shrugged. "It was Garrett's idea. He always came up with these crazy schemes and usually I was the only one who would go along with them."

"That's funny. I like it. We could do that if you want," she said, smiling at him. "When the Candied Apple & Café was under construction, we used to go down to the Ralph Lauren Polo store on 5th Avenue and get coffee and use their bathroom—they are so clean. Anyway, when one of the managers noticed we were coming in there a lot to use the facilities and asked if we lived or worked nearby, Iona gave her a haughty stare and said "don't you know who we are?" She kind of stared at us and then slowly nodded. For weeks afterward she treated us like we were some kind of celeb … it was sort of funny, but mostly embarrassing."

"I can't see you enjoying that at all," Hoop said. Considering that Hayley preferred to blend in most of the time.

"I mostly hated it, but a part of me secretly enjoyed it. When the Candied Apple & Café opened, Hayley and I sent the staff a huge hamper of chocolate and a thank you note for being so generous to us."

"So Central Park it is. Plus, it's close to your place in case the heat gets too much and you need to go home," he said, giving her a way out.

"It is hot today," Cici agreed as they left the yacht and he hailed a cab. She pulled a pair of large framed sunglasses from her bag and put them on. Her skin looked flush and a bead of sweat dripped down from her forehead.

He held the door for her and she slipped past him on a wave of summery scents, coconut mingling with the salty sea air. He closed his eyes and remembered the first time he'd gone to the beach and how he'd never wanted to leave.

"Hoop?" she asked.

"Yeah, sorry. I was distracted."

She slid across the seat and he got in beside her. Was he chasing after her because she had something that had always eluded him? There was attraction between them of course but now that she was pregnant she was the complete package. Being with Cici was like getting a ready-made family.

"I haven't spent that much time in the City when I'm not working," she admitted. "We are always at our cottage in Sag Harbor. My mom works from home over the summer and when we were growing up Steve used to have Saturdays off. We spent long days in the sand and water."

"That sounds really nice," he said. "We did the same. Are you going to stay in the city once you have your baby?"

She shrugged. "I haven't really thought beyond admitting to myself and others that I am pregnant. I think I've been hoping by not talking about it I'll stay in a bubble and not have to figure out the future. I mean, I know that Hayley and Iona won't mind if I bring the baby into work with me. But that's just a temporary solution … I have a lot to figure out."

"My mom always says that you don't have to do it all in one

day. That life is going to keep on moving and you can figure out all of it one piece at a time."

"Very wise," Cici said. "She sounds wonderful."

"She is," Hoop said. And she was. He was very aware of how lucky he was to call her mom.

"That's one of the things that's bothers me … I'm smart at certain things but I'm not wise and I'm not … well, 'mom-like'. You know. I spend more time worrying about my eyebrows being on fleek than my mom ever has. I mean, beyond getting hers waxed I doubt she's ever thought of them. I feel like this baby means I'm going to have to start being … someone else."

"I tried to order furniture for the nursery but the decorator had a bunch of questions and I finally had to leave with the promise to come back with a vision board … I mean a vision board? Really? I just wanted something that would make my baby feel comforted and happy."

She glanced over at Hoop and he was watching her like her brothers did sometimes … like they thought the conversation was too girly and didn't know how to respond. She knew she should stop talking and abruptly shut her mouth. What was wrong with her today?

"How about a beach theme?" Hoop suggested. "Or wherever it is that makes you feel most at home. For me, it's being on the water. And it could work for a boy or girl … if you had girl you could do some sort of mermaids and if it's a boy boats and maybe mermen?"

Hoop.

He'd changed the dynamic between them. Becoming lovers hadn't changed the fact that he was still her friend. Spontaneously, she reached over and hugged him.

"What was that for?"

"Being you," she said. "I need to think more like that."

Her concerns about being a mother were legit. She hadn't been

102

joking when she'd been spewing all that stuff about eyebrows and the fact that when she thought about any advice she'd given to anyone lately, it wasn't wise. Not like a mother's. Instead, it was more sorority sister stuff. Like the new Lilly print that had been released or the best place to get a lobster roll on Long Island. She'd been in the shop when a customer had asked and she knew a good place…

"I think that when the time comes you will find the wise words," Hoop said as the cab pulled to a stop at Central Park near the boathouse. She took her wallet out but Hoop already had the cash in his hand. She opened her door and stepped out onto the sidewalk. It was hot. Even dressed as she was for summer, she still felt like it was oppressive. Being in the park would be nicer since there was some shade and green and the air was at times cooler than it was here on the street.

Hoop adjusted his baseball cap as he started walking into the park. She walked next to him, thinking that to the world they might look like a couple. *A real couple.* And that made her happy for a few moments. She hadn't been part of a couple in a long time. Mainly down to the fact that she hadn't wanted a regular guy in her life.

"What are you thinking?"

She chewed on her lower lip and he arched one eyebrow at her. "Just trying to ascertain if you really want to know. Remember the last time I started talking and couldn't stop."

He just shook his head and lifted his hands. "It's a risk I'm willing to take."

She smiled. "Okay, then … I was thinking we looked like a real couple."

"Aren't we?" he asked.

She shrugged. "I seem to keep getting us into these discussions, which hasn't ever been my intention. I mean, of course we're a couple. We slept together, we're … dating? Are we dating?"

"Yes, we're dating. So, what does it mean when you say "real"?"

103

"Oh, now I feel stupid," she admitted. "I meant on the outside we look like we don't have any issues or problems."

"On the outside?" he asked.

"Yeah, you know. No one knows I screwed up my first shot with you or that I'm pregnant … or any of the other junk. We just look like a cute couple."

There was a long pause and Hoop took her hand, drawing her to a stop underneath the branches of a thick tree and he pulled her into his arms. He put his hands on her waist and stared down into her eyes. His gaze was so intense she caught her breath.

"For the record … no one is perfect," he said. "And I like the way our story is unraveling."

"You do?" she asked surprised, putting her arms around his waist and then unable to her help herself, she hugged him tightly and rested her head against his chest. It was nice to just have someone hold her like this. To hold Hoop in return. It was something she hadn't realized she wanted until this moment.

"Hmm mmm," he said. Then he tipped her chin up and leaned down and kissed her gently. There was that spark of awareness arching between them but more than that, there was comfort and caring.

She almost thought … Hoop liked her. It didn't seem to matter if she wasn't wise or if she was a bit cowardly. "I'm not perfect either."

But he was.

He was perfect in ways that she was just beginning to see and was still struggling to understand. But he was definitely a good man. And more than anything, she wanted to make sure she never hurt him.

"Let's go," she said, turning out of his arms and jogging toward the boathouse. What was wrong with her today?

Was this the pregnancy hormones she'd read about in the book? Or was she just losing it?

She heard him next to her and then he smacked her on the butt as he passed her. "Last one there has to row."

She shook her head and started running faster. The athlete in her rising to the surface. She hated to lose. She pushed, her legs pumping harder and for the first time since she woke up this morning she stopped thinking. Her mind was focused on running and on beating Hoop and as they rounded the corner, both swerving to avoid a family that had stopped in the middle of the path, she got a burst of energy and touched the door to the boathouse a millisecond before Hoop.

He started laughing. And she couldn't help it as she joined in. The laughter made it easy to believe that her doubts about motherhood would pass as quickly as her fears had just now. That maybe moving forward was the key to getting through this. She couldn't stay mired in the past.

She'd known that for years but now it actually mattered.

"Guess you'll get a chance to show off those guns of yours," she said with a wink. "I'm going to get some water while you rent us a boat. I'll get you some too."

She walked away to the nearby concession stand.

"You two are such a cute couple," the lady behind her in line said. "My husband and I used to do things like that."

She smiled at the woman who looked to be her age, maybe a year or two older. "Thanks. Why don't you do that anymore?"

She shrugged. "Kids I guess. They take all of our time and energy."

Cici ordered their drinks and smiled and waved goodbye to the lady, trying to keep her newfound happiness front of mind.

An afternoon rowing and then ice cream after had mellowed him out … well the run had changed him. It had made him disconnect from the childhood fears that Cici had stirred up. That feeling of not being any good or worthy. It was something he'd believed he'd left behind a long time ago so he wasn't too pleased to realize he hadn't.

"You're very good on the water," she said as they were walking through Central Park toward the amphitheater where Shakespeare in the Park was held.

"Thanks … I try," he said. "You were a pretty bossy passenger."

She shrugged and looked at him over her shoulder. "I wanted to make sure you were doing it properly."

"Thank goodness you were there," he said. "Actually, as bossy as you are I bet you won't have any problem being a mom."

"Yeah, giving orders isn't the problem," she said.

"You'll get it all sorted."

"Speaking of sorting things out. I wanted to talk to you for your lawyer's perspective. I sent a message to Rich and haven't heard back from him but I expect to any day. I have an address for his parents' house, but I would rather not send it to them," she said. "I guess I'm not sure if we should use his family's address or search for a Los Angeles one?"

"Not a problem. If you have his full name, Lilia's assistant will be able to find him," Hoop said. "We do that all the time."

Today had driven home the fact that she wanted to have everything with Rich resolved. She was starting to fall for Hoop and she couldn't move on, not really, until she knew what involvement, if any, Rich and his family would have in her baby's life.

"You okay?" he asked after a few minutes.

"Yeah, why?" she replied. She felt sort of calm as if she should be worried about something but there was nothing to worry about.

"You seem different. When we were running … well you seemed to let go and now you are hiding again."

She flushed, bit her lower lip and then looked away from him. He rubbed the back of his neck and wondered what kind of crap he'd done in a previous life to make this one so damned complicated. He couldn't fall for a woman more complex than Cici. She was the good friend of his best-friend's fiancée, she was pregnant with another man's child and she made him feel more alive than any other woman ever had.

She stirred those longings for things he didn't like to admit he needed. Family … one of his own. One that no one could say he was lucky to have, but one that was just his. He wondered if it was simply that Garrett had settled down that was making him want something permanent. But he'd never been that kind of a man and he knew it was because of Cici.

"I am. That lady, when I got the water she said we looked like a cute couple and mentioned she and her hubby had been like that before kids. And it made me realize that you are going to have to deal with a lot of stuff that is beyond what dating should be."

Hoop took Cici's hand and drew her closer to him. She smelled of summer and sweat but it was sweet. So sweet. He was a goner where she was concerned and he wasn't too sure that was a good thing because Cici was in flux. She wasn't close to being certain of anything at this moment. Which made it dangerous for him to allow her into his life. But he couldn't push her away. Not now.

He pushed a tendril of hair behind her ear and leaned down, resting his forehead against her. Behind her glasses, she had thick eyelashes and the breath when she exhaled was warm against his lips and minty.

He kissed her.

He meant for it to be soft and gentle but instead some of the desperation he felt made its way into the embrace and he thrust his tongue deep into her mouth, claiming her in the one way he could. He marked her as his. He took everything she had to give and when he lifted his head, her eyes were closed and her face was flushed.

She was breathing a little bit heavier and she clung to his hips with her hands, keeping him close when he would have stepped away.

"Nothing in my life has ever been what it *should* be," he admitted. "You could say this is par for the course and Cici, babe, I can't walk away right now. Things might get too much at some point but this is our first day together as a couple and I'm not a quitter."

"I'm not either," she said.

"Good," he replied. "How about I take you to dinner and then get you home so you are ready for work tomorrow?"

"Sounds good."

They had dinner and Hoop vacillated between thinking that the date was going well and the belief that they were both faking it. Both afraid to admit they might have made a mistake when they said they could handle this. For himself, he'd fallen in love with different families in his past and been hurt and broken when they were just temporary. And he had to remember that Cici hadn't committed to anything other than dating him.

Dating.

Nothing more.

He kissed her goodnight at her front door and then watched the doorman hold the door for her before he turned to walk away. He told himself he was strong enough to handle whatever came his way but when he rounded the corner and hailed a cab to go back to his place, he knew he wasn't. That just once he wanted what seemed to come so easily to everyone else.

He wanted the girl, the baby Cici was carrying and the happily-ever-after. But he was pragmatic enough to know that it wouldn't be that easy.

Chapter 11

Hoop got to the office early. Spending the entire day with Cici had been good but when she'd left to go home it had awakened feelings he'd thought he'd outgrown. Those feelings that he'd left in boyhood when he'd been in the foster system. Before he'd come to live with his Ma and Pops.

Loneliness.

For so many years he'd only relied on himself and even though he had siblings and good friends he always kept a part of himself isolated from them. A part of himself tucked away from the bonds with those others so that he wouldn't be disappointed when they left.

He got it. There was something about starting a new relationship and that headlong rush of wanting to be with the other person all the time. But this was different. This *felt* different.

Cici's scent was on his clothes and even after he'd left his yacht and gone to his apartment, he couldn't shake her. He'd watched ESPN and read up on the case that Martin brought him in on and it distracted him for a while. He wanted to prove himself and he would. This was something he was good at. And for a few hours he forgot about his personal life.

But still it was Cici on his mind as he'd gone to bed.

Cici and her baby.

In the past, he'd just go out with the guys to distract himself, but Garrett had Hayley now and the rest of the guys from the precinct were on duty. He wished he'd made some friends at the law office but everyone was like him. They worked all the time and in their downtime, whatever they had, they stayed away from anything to do with the office.

So here he was at five-thirty in the morning on the treadmill at the office gym. He should be thinking about the junior partnership. He had a huge case load but instead of reviewing that he was wondering if a family was always going to be just out of his grasp.

He ran harder as the program he'd selected went on an incline but even the air burning in his lungs couldn't shake the thought that maybe he was one of those people who was always on the outside looking in.

He knew the Fillions had adopted him and made him their own but a part of him always felt like he knew the truth. He wasn't one of theirs and no matter how much he wanted it to be different, he couldn't change that. Sometimes, when he looked in the mirror, he wondered who his ancestors were. Had he inherited the cut of his jaw from his father, were those his mother's eyes? But there were no answers.

He was a solitary man and most of the time that didn't bother him.

Damn.

He needed to get out of his head. To stop obsessing so much. But he couldn't. When he closed his eyes, he saw Cici and thought about the baby growing inside of her. He wanted to be a part of her life but he'd never seen himself as a father.

Honestly, his work with Big Brothers satisfied his need to be a role model and to be there for kids who didn't have anyone. But being a father ... no.

That wasn't a role he'd ever wanted for himself and if he

was being totally honest, he wasn't sure he knew how to be one.

Sure, Pops was a good example when he'd been a teenager but there were a lot of years between birth and teen. And Hoop didn't know if he had the guts to do it.

He finished his running program, showered and went up to his office. He looked out at the road below, quiet in the early morning except for a few pedestrians and the odd taxi. The city looked the way he felt.

He was on a one-way track to depression and no one liked that. Not him. Not his family and certainly not his bosses.

He picked up the phone; he needed to make plans. Plans without Cici. That was his problem. He'd been focused on seducing her. On sating that desire he'd had for her from the moment they'd met.

He could check that off now and step back. Try to regain the focus that was sadly lacking in his life right now.

He dialed Garrett's number.

"Dude, it's not even seven," Garrett said.

"Hayley gets up at five to get to the shop and make candy. I know you're not sleeping," Hoop responded.

"True. What's up?" Garrett asked.

"I've got tickets to the Nicks game tonight. Wanna join me?"

There was a pause. "You sure you want my company?"

"Yeah. I could take one of my little brothers if you don't want to," Hoop said.

"Nah, I'm good. Hayley said I'm turning into a homebody."

"You are," Hoop said, trying to ignore the pang in his soul. A part of him wanted that life.

"Speaking of which, we're grilling out on Saturday. Can you make it?" Garrett asked.

"Uh, no. I kind of told Cici I'd go with her to the Hamptons this weekend. I invited her to come to my folks place on the Fourth. But this is just going to be us."

"Alright! I was hoping you two would hook up."

"She's more than a hook up," Hoop said.

"Even better. I think she'll be good for you," Garrett said. "Plus, I have the feeling Hayley has been rooting for you two. She keeps coming up with events that we could host and can casually invite you both to."

Hoop had to laugh at that. Hayley had been helping him out indirectly and directly to help his cause with Cici. But now that he had her, he wasn't too sure what the next steps were.

And that wasn't like him. He was a man of action. This indecision was pissing him off.

He knew it was because for the first time since he'd come to the Fillions' house, he was starting to see his future with another person and that scared him.

"See you tonight," Hoop said and disconnected the call.

He needed a long day of family law to take his mind off Cici and the family he was building in his head.

Calling her mom should have been a no brainer. They weren't as close as Cici would have liked and the fact was she just didn't want to tell her.

But Hoop had been right when he said the more time she let pass, the worse it would seem. Her mom's reaction wasn't going to be any better if Cici called her six months from now and told her she was pregnant. She had to get it over with.

Like ripping off the band aid, she'd just do it.

She texted her mom to see if she was home and if she could talk. Her parents had a house in Queens and then the cottage in Sag Harbor that her mom had purchased with the money she'd gotten from her father's death benefit. The house technically speaking belonged to Cici and her mom only but Cici always thought of it as the family place.

Her mom called instead of texting back, which Cici should have anticipated.

"Hey."

"Are you okay?" her mom asked. "I expected to see you last weekend."

Guilt. She sighed. "Sorry, Mom, I … I'm fine … I, well, the reason I haven't been home is that I've been trying to figure out how to tell you something. And there's not an easy way to say it."

"What is it? Is it the business?" her mom asked.

She took a deep breath. "I'm pregnant."

"What? Are you dating someone? How come we haven't met him? Why would you hide …"

"Mom. Stop. It's nothing like that. I made a mistake and slept with one of the groomsmen at Stacey's wedding. And I'm pregnant."

There was silence on the line and to Cici it seemed loud and long.

"Okay. Well, is the guy … what's his name?" her mom asked.

"Rich Maguire. He's originally from somewhere in New England but lives in LA now. He's involved with someone else and doesn't want to be a part of the baby's life. I'm trying to sort that out."

"What can I do?" her mom said. "Are you excited about the baby?"

She put her hand on her stomach. "I am, Mom. At first, I was in denial but now, I am getting more attached."

"That's good. Wow, I'm going to be a grandma."

"Yes, you are," Cici said.

How far along are you?"

"Fourteen weeks," she said.

"I'm going to come into the city and take you to dinner so we can talk some more."

"Thanks, Mom. I'm sorry I didn't tell you before," Cici said.

"Don't be. I can tell from your voice that things have been hectic. I'm going to get changed and then I'll head in. Should I

113

come to your place or the Candied Apple & Café?"

Cici glanced at the clock. It was three in the afternoon and Hayley was teaching one of her candy making classes that evening. "The Candied Apple & Café."

She hung up the phone and felt … well, a little bit lighter. The burden—that wasn't really the right word for—but the secrecy of the pregnancy had been weighing on her. She'd isolated herself from her friends and family and only Hoop knew as much as he did because … well, she liked him and he'd been easy to talk to.

And a part of her realized she'd wanted to tell him. In her mind he'd been a part of the journey from the beginning. He'd been the one she'd wanted and thought about and if she were being totally honest, the man she'd substituted for Rich that night in Jamaica.

"Cici?" Hayley said from the doorway. "You okay? Is something wrong with the baby?"

She lifted her head and looked at her friend. Hayley leaned against the doorframe with her arms crossed over her chest.

"You ever have one of those moments when you realize something that was there all along and you get why you were ignoring it?" Cici asked.

"All the time. Sometimes with the candy I create in the kitchen. Always with my dad and occasionally with Garrett. I'm pretty much running around like a crazy woman inside my head 24/7."

Cici smiled at the image. "You are the least crazy person I know."

"On the outside," Hayley said, coming in to sit on the edge of Cici's desk. She reached over, pushing a strand of Cici's hair behind her ear. "Give yourself a break. You're pregnant. It's summer and danged hot. And you are secretly dating someone."

"What?"

"Don't even try to pretend. Garrett called Hoop last night and he spilled the entire thing."

Crap.

"It's not that I wasn't going to tell you," Cici started.

"It's okay, Ci. I would keep it quiet too. I'm sorry for my part in making dating him odd," Hayley said.

"That's just it, Hay. It's not odd. I wish it were, and then maybe I'd feel better about everything. He's just so … Hoop. Nothing seems to really shake him," she said, but she knew that wasn't true. She'd seen his face yesterday morning when she'd returned to his yacht. He'd been dazed when she'd left him.

"I'm here. If you want to talk about anything," Hayley said. "I like Hoop, but I love you. You're my heart sister and I don't want you to ever feel like you're isolated."

"I don't," Cici said. "My main problem is me."

"How?"

"I'm just … in flux. You know when you're making a new truffle for the store and make us sample about a hundred different flavor combos?"

"Well I think a hundred is an exaggeration, but yes," Hayley said.

"My life is like that right now. There are all these different combinations of things I could do and be and I know that until this little bean is born," she said, touching her stomach, "I won't know what it's going to be. But I hate that. It's not that I'm a control freak, but I want to make a plan, pick the best option and just be sure that I haven't chosen poorly."

"One thing that my mom said in her last letter to me was that there are no wrong choices in our lives. We take the path and we walk it. You can do that, Cici. Whatever you choose, it will be awesome because *you* are."

She wanted to believe Hayley and her heart was heavy with the love she felt for her friend. She was glad to know that someone was behind her and thought she hadn't already messed everything up.

Hannah Johnson still looked young, despite the fact that she was in her late 40s. Cici's mom had three kids, a good marriage and a job that she loved. Growing up, there were times when Cici and Hannah hadn't gotten along, but she always knew her mom loved her.

It was simply that she'd always wanted Cici to see Steve as her dad and hadn't wanted to talk about Cici's biological father, something that could be an issue with her own relationship with her child. She wanted to do it better than her mom had, but really had no idea how.

Today was no different as they crossed the street and entered Central Park. It was late afternoon, summer, so the park was busy with families running and laughing and tourists who were enjoying the shade provided by the trees in this leafy green oasis.

Her mom looped her arm through Cici's and they turned to the left and started following the path that would eventually lead them around in a big circle. Neither woman said anything and in her mind Cici knew she should start the conversation but she wasn't sure how to.

"So …" her mom said at last.

"Yeah, about this. What do you want to know?" she asked her mom tentatively.

"Whatever you want to share," her mom said. She kept the pace leisurely and Cici realized, not for the first time, that her mom never hurried.

"Why aren't you ever hurrying around?" she asked. A little to stall the inevitable questions but also because so many moms she knew were always rushing. They seemed to be behind all the time but her mom never had been.

"Why would I be? There's plenty of time in the day to accomplish all that needs doing," she said. "You know that."

"I do. But I always feel like if I don't have a plan I won't get to it all," she said.

"That's Steve's attitude too. You must have picked it up from him," her mom said.

She hated when her mom did that. Steve wasn't her dad. Didn't her mom realize that? "Maybe it came from my dad. You've never really talked too much about him. Just showed me the old pictures."

"I know," her mom said. "I didn't want you to dwell too much on what was missing. Does that make sense?"

In a way it did. But it had also sharpened her curiosity about her biological father. "I guess."

"Now that you are going to be a mom, you will see what I'm talking about. Every day, you just do the best you can and hope that you haven't screwed up too much."

"Mom, you didn't screw up with me," she said. "I wish I had planned to be pregnant, I think my mindset would be better."

Her mom led them over to an empty bench and they both sat down. "Honey, there is no guarantee that a planned pregnancy is going to be any smoother than an unplanned one."

Cici held her breath and waited. Would her mom talk about her father? After all this time.

"Your dad and I had it all worked out. We got married, waited a year to build up our savings and buy our own place and then I got pregnant and two days after I found out, your dad got orders and left … all those plans we'd made were gone. And after that … well I stopped making those kind of plans," her mom said.

"Why?"

"Because planning like that doesn't make life smoother. In fact, I think it makes life harder. I tried to force us back on the path we'd mapped out before he left and it never worked. When your dad died, I was free falling. I had a baby girl that I'd planned to stay home and raise and now I had to work. You'd never been with a sitter and you didn't like strangers. I honestly was so freaked out, honey. Some nights, when you woke up crying, I just held you and cried with you."

Cici hugged her mom. She had never realized that the woman

who seemed to always know what she was doing had ever had doubts. These were real crises of confidence that Cici herself was experiencing every day.

"Mom, I had no idea."

"Good, I'm glad. And you know what, honey, your baby won't either," her mom said. "No matter what happens, as long as you love your baby that's all they remember."

Cici swallowed hard, thinking about her little bean and knowing how much she loved this baby. She felt a certain sense of rightness to what her mother had said.

"Now, tell me about the father."

"He's out of the picture. I'm not going to name him because he told me he wants no part in the child's life."

"Did you know that before?" her mom asked.

"Mom, it was a one-night stand. Neither of us meant for anything to happen. I drank too much. I know, you have always told me to be careful," she said.

"I'm not going to judge you," her mom said. "Mostly, I give you advice like that so you won't make mistakes like I have."

She smiled at her mom. "Thanks. I think I needed to hear that."

"Hear what?"

"That you aren't superwoman."

"Well let's not get carried away, I'm still pretty awesome," her mom said with a wink. "But I am human just like you. What's next? You said you're dating someone."

"Next is … well, tied to who I'm dating. He's a great guy, a friend of Hayley's fiancé. He's a lawyer and he suggested I have the father sign a waiver of paternity. I've hired an attorney and we have the paperwork all ready to go but the father won't respond to my texts or anything. And I wanted to give him a head's up before I just sent the paperwork to him."

Her mom nodded. "Want me or Steve to do it for you? I wouldn't mind."

No way. Her mom was very protective of all of them and Cici had a feeling that if Hannah got Rich on the phone she'd give him a stinging lecture about walking away. "Thanks, Mom, but I need to do this myself."

"Fair enough," her mom said. "But if you change your mind."

"I know you're right here."

"That's right. Now about the guy you're dating …"

"It's complicated."

"When isn't it," her mom said with a laugh. "Come on, let's walk some more and you can tell me all about him."

They walked through the park, stopping at an ice cream vendor to get lemon ice and Cici told her mom about Hoop. And as she talked she realized how great a guy he was and how afraid she was that she'd do something to hurt him.

Chapter 12

Two weeks later Rich finally answered her and it was only after she'd told him she didn't want any money, that she just wanted some guarantees that he wouldn't be in the child's life once she had the baby.

She and Hoop were getting closer but their jobs kept them both very busy. He'd gone to Sag Harbor with her and met her parents and the twins who were enjoying their last summer of freedom before starting their senior year in college. And Cici's mom had given her a box of baby stuff that Cici had never seen before. It contained some things from her biological father including a child's rocking chair that Cici remembered from her childhood bedroom. She'd been touched by it.

She'd noticed that Hoop had been quiet after they'd gotten home and they'd only had dinner together once but had texted a few times since. Her phone pinged as she arrived at the office.

Hoop: *Are you free for dinner on Saturday?*

Cici: *Yes. Come to my place I'll cook.*

Hoop: *Sounds good. Seven?*

Cici: *See you then.*

She put her phone on her desk and turned back to her

computer. But the truth was, for once numbers weren't the solace they always had been.

Maybe because the numbers were relentless. She'd had 280 days to get ready for something that she doubted she'd be ready for if she had double that many. And it was already done 130 days.

She was making progress at least with getting Rich legally out of the picture. She doubted very much that he would suddenly show back up in her life. She had the feeling that, like herself, he had sort of put their one night together down to island fever and regret. She wondered how his family would feel about that. And she was honest enough with herself to admit she wanted to find out if they were interested in meeting the baby.

"Are the financials that bad?" Iona asked from the doorway.

She had her red hair pulled back into a high ponytail and her sunglasses were pushed up on the top of her head.

"They are actually really good. I think the additional classes are going to pay for the refurbishment of the space upstairs by the end of the next quarter. We are doing really well with them," Cici said.

"Good," Iona said as she walked into the office, sat down on one of the guest chairs and crossed her legs. "My mom wants me to go to Greece and find a nice boy."

Cici leaned back in her chair and admitted that she was glad to have someone else's life to worry about for a few moments. Plus, Iona was usually so strong with everyone except her mother. "Tell her no."

"I did. But she said I'm not really looking here and … she's persistent, Cici. I can't figure out how to get her off my back without hurting her feelings," Iona said.

"Fake boyfriend?" Cici suggested. Someday, was her kiddo going to be talking to friends about her like this? She hoped not but the truth was Iona's mom was a good one … is that what being a good mother was about? Being in her kid's business all the time?

"Fake one. Are you kidding me, Cici? I need a real solution, not something you saw on a soap," Iona said.

And for the first time, Cici realized something was going on with Io. Something more than she'd appreciated.

"I was joking," Cici said. "What is really going on? You can say no to a trip to Greece; the store is busy and we need you here, something like that."

Iona rubbed the back of her neck. "Sorry I snapped at you. I think my yia-yia has hired a matchmaker. Mom sorted of hinted that this time I'd come back with a man."

Cici knew that Iona had been feeling the pressure to settle down. She was thirty, they all were this year, and her family had been willing to let her find her own path but they wanted more Greek babies. Something that Iona's mom said to her frequently. "Okay, so don't go. Don't meet the matchmaker."

"You're right, but another part of me …" she leaned back in the chair and closed Cici's office door and then looked back over at her. "A part of me is ready to settle down. You're having a kid, Hayley's engaged and I'm over here hooking up with guys who are fun, which is great but I don't know how to find a guy for the long haul."

Cici stood up and walked around her desk, perched on the side of Iona's chair and wrapped her arm around her friend. "No one knows how to find one of those. Do you want them to find you a guy?"

Iona shrugged. "No. Most days the answer is no, but you know I don't want to spend my entire life single. I always thought someday I'd meet someone and settle down but that hasn't happened. Part of it is me, you know I have high standards."

Cici laughed. "The highest … I don't know what to tell you to do. Whatever you decide, I've got your back."

"I know you do. I guess I was thinking since you are sort of in the middle of …"

"A mess?" Cici asked.

"Not a mess. You are in the middle of figuring out your life and I thought maybe you'd be able to give me some advice."

Cici felt something shift and settle inside of her. "Thanks, Io, that means a lot to me. I don't know what to tell you except that I ran from Hoop as hard as I could and I ended up back here trying to figure out something with him. I think that we can't run from our chosen path, you know. That no matter what you decide, if this matchmaker, your yia-yia, has named a man for you and it's meant to be, he will find you."

Iona's idea for escaping was a day at the spa. They hit the Red Door Spa. They had relaxing massages and then manicures and pedicures while talking about nothing and just laughing and having fun. For the first time in a long while, Cici didn't really worry about not being enough. With Io she always was.

She looked over at her friend who was busy texting someone on her phone. For the first time, she was seeing the chinks in Iona's perfect life. She'd always sort of envied Io and believed out of the three of them she was the one who was the most successful at life. Hayley was good in the kitchen and that was where she focused her attention and she really excelled, hiding away from the world making her dreamy, chocolatey confections. Cici, herself put everything into columns and sorted them, adding and subtracting things until everything balanced … until the baby and Hoop. But Iona … she just always mastered everything. She was the one who seemed to know how to breeze through life.

And Cici realized she'd taken her friend at face value.

"Want to see Hamilton tonight?"

"Are you kidding me?! I've been trying to get tickets for months," Cici said. She thought fleetingly of her plans with Hoop but surely he'd understand this was Hamilton. Also, she worried a little bit that she relied on him too much. That she was making him into her life to help bridge the gap between the life she knew and the one she had to make.

"Not kidding. My mom is trying to bribe me to go to Greece," Iona said. "Dad apparently knows someone … though why we couldn't have gotten tickets early is beyond me."

"Io, if we go do you have to go to Greece?" Cici asked. "If so, then my answer is no."

Iona put her phone on the counter and turned to face her and in her blue eyes Cici saw something she hadn't seen in her friend ever before. Resignation. It was as if she had given up and she wondered if everyone saw that in her own eyes. She was losing herself and it was only the first trimester. She needed to figure out motherhood. She didn't want anyone to look at her like she was looking at Iona and feel … pity.

"I'm going. I already decided. It's like you said. Fate can't be changed. Hoop ran from you and now you two are dating. Cosmic karma."

She shook her head. Though she knew that Iona was superstitious, Cici had always been a cold-hard-give-me-proof sort of person. Numbers added up to something. Coincidences didn't. They were random.

"Are you sure about that? I think I just said that earlier to make myself feel better. You know, since I got pregnant, I've felt like I have no control over my life. I'm trying to adjust to the consequences of having made a poor choice and it makes me feel stupid that I ever thought … well, that sleeping with another man would resolve what I was feeling about Hoop."

Iona shook her head and then started laughing. "Oh my God, you sound like what's going on in my head. It's like I'm on a crazy train that is running out of control and I can't figure out how to get off. I mean, my mom isn't going to give up on matching me with someone. I figure the best way for me to take control is to meet her guy and then reject him."

Cici smiled. Best laid plans. That was what ran through her head. She'd fallen into bed with Rich to forget. She hadn't fooled herself that he was trying to forget someone as well. They'd both sort of figured they'd do this thing and move on and look what had happened.

But Iona was scared. Cici didn't know why but her friend spent a lot of time being very careful not to let anyone get too close. She was sure that there were secrets Iona kept even from her and Hayley.

She also didn't have a solution for Iona so it was best to back her friend's plan and be there for her if it didn't work out. That was what she was coming to realize about life. That plans weren't worth the time. She had thought she was in control and Hoop threw all that out the window.

"Sounds good. We can go to Hamilton guilt free?"

Iona nodded. "Yes and you can bring a date. Or maybe Hayley."

"Do you have a date?" Cici asked.

"Uh, yeah. Mom already has the guy yia-yia's matchmaker found lined up."

"You want me there to vet him?" Cici asked. Who was this guy that the matchmaker had found for Iona. She had never really thought much about finding her perfect man.

"Sort of. Will you do it?" Iona asked.

"Yes," Cici said. "And if Hoop can't make it I'll go with your brother," Cici said.

Iona nodded. "Thanks."

"Girl, that's what friends are for," Cici said. She texted Hoop to see if he could make the 8pm curtain. He texted back immediately saying yes.

She noticed she also had a missed call from her attorney. Which worried her.

"We can go," Cici said.

"Great," Iona replied.

"I have to call my attorney," Cici said. "I'll be right back."

She left the spa and went into a private area and dialed Lilia's number.

"Cici, thanks for returning my call," Lilia said. "It seems Rich

126

didn't give you his full name. He is part of the Hallifax family and our firm already represents him."

"What does that mean?"

"Just that I'm going to be going up against one of our other attorneys … actually one of the partners. The Hallifax family is one of her largest clients. I wanted to give you a head's up. I saw your text messages with Rich, which will give us a place to start from, but it might not be as straightforward as we'd hoped. I'll keep you posted."

Nico Marinos didn't seem like the kind of man who had to have a matchmaker find him a date. But then Iona had never been to one so she had no idea what special qualities they might have. He was handsome in that Mediterranean way that Greek men had. He was tanned and well dressed. He spoke English with a British accent and he and Hoop had bonded over boats. Seemed Nico designed some of the most expensive yachts in the world.

Iona's date was the perfect distraction from waiting to hear back from her attorney. She should have guessed Rich had lied to her about his name. And she was anxious because even she had heard of the Hallifax family. They were involved in shipping and politics. They were a dynasty like the Kennedys had been and she was sending them something that said they gave up all rights to her baby.

The men went out at intermission to get drinks and Cici and Iona stood to stretch their legs. The musical was beyond good but tonight she just couldn't concentrate on it.

"He doesn't seem that bad," Cici said. It was hard to find fault with a man who had all those white teeth and the kind of winning grin that Hollywood would totally eat up.

"Sure, he's nice enough now but that's probably because he wants to make a good first impression," Iona said. "He does smell good."

Cici smiled and then said, "One thing in his favor. And he has a good job."

"Cici, stop trying to sell me on him. He's too hot to need a matchmaker. "

"Maybe he's picky like you," Cici pointed out, arching her eyebrow at her friend.

Iona tapped her long fingernail against her teeth. "It's like my mom described the exact perfect man for me. Makes me think that there must be something that all that eye candy is there to distract me from."

"Like what?" Cici asked. "I'm not being difficult but, like, Rich was good looking but he was on the rebound from some relationship that had him torn up. Is that what you mean?"

Iona nodded and then shook her head. "Yes, just like that. We've both binge watched Millionaire Matchmakers on TV. It's not unbelievable that a man with a lot of money would need help with women but he's pretty charming."

"Who is?" Nico asked as he rejoined them, handing Iona her glass of champagne.

Cici felt herself flushing as she realized he'd overheard their conversation. Hoop handed her a plastic glass with sparkling water in it and draped his arm over her shoulder and she looked up at him smiling. There was something so nice about having someone to lean on.

"You," Iona said. "I'm not going to apologize for wondering why you used a matchmaker."

Ballsy as always, Cici turned her head into Hoop's chest to hide her laughter. Hoop rubbed his hand on her back and when she looked up at him he was smiling. It was the first time she'd seen him this way. He was totally relaxed and it made her feel good inside.

"Why did you?" Nico asked.

"My mom did," Iona said. "Oh, great. That makes me sound worse than you."

He laughed and Cici noticed that Iona smiled when he did. Her friend was attracted to her blind date. Nico wore a pair of dress pants and a button-down shirt with an attractive print on it. He'd left the first three buttons undone revealing a gold medallion and a small bit of chest hair. He had eyes the color of the Aegean Sea and his hair was black as midnight and well styled.

He was cute, but he didn't make her heart race the way Hoop did.

Hoop wore a pair of dark wash jeans and a striped oxford style shirt that he'd left only the top button undone on. His shirt was untucked and his brown hair was a little bit mussed, which she knew was because he ran his fingers through his hair when he was reading. She'd noticed it when they'd been on his yacht.

She glanced up at him and felt that swell of emotion that she was afraid to name. It was the same swell of emotion she'd experienced for the first time in Olympus when she'd met him and danced with him. She knew she was falling for him. Hadn't stopped falling for him from the moment they met.

He winked at her and squeezed her close to him.

"Nothing could make you sound bad," Nico said and there was a tone in his voice that made her realize that he liked Iona as well.

"Wait until you hear her dressing down someone," Cici said, smiling.

"She's right. I can be a full-on diva at times," Iona admitted.

"I'm told I can be a shark at times," Nico said.

The lights flicked and they all turned to sit back down. Hoop leaned over to Cici and she closed her eyes as she inhaled his earthy aftershave.

"I like him. He doesn't seem awed by Iona, which is what I've noticed most men tend to be," Hoop said.

"I like him too. He's definitely not her usual kind of man," Cici whispered back. "I think he might be just what she needs."

He draped his arm over the back of her seat and she settled

into the curve of his body, once again realizing how easily he made her not feel alone. She told herself not to get used to it. That he wanted to talk to her, that he wanted to discuss something. But right now, that didn't matter.

"What about me?" he asked.

"What about you?"

"Am *I* what you need?" he asked.

She took a deep breath. Fear keeping her words in the back of her throat. She was scared to admit to him how much she was coming to rely on him. Just for emotional support and for this … but it didn't change the truth she knew deep in her soul.

"Yes," she admitted. "You are."

While the second act of Hamilton got underway with its message and hip hop songs resonating in her mind, she didn't think of anything except the moment. This was what she'd been struggling with. Life was made of moments, not of plans. She had to remember that.

Chapter 13

Hoop wished he was out on his yacht tonight instead of sitting in the dark theatre with Cici. He wanted Cici by his side and he wanted to be charting a course away from Manhattan, get her out of this place. He liked that they were on a date with her friend. It was odd to think of Iona being set up, but then nothing in life was as it seemed. He knew that.

Cici was singing along to the song on the stage, a reprise of One Shot, and he felt just like Alexander Hamilton; a man who had carved his own place for himself in the world. But Hamilton had the confidence to take what he wanted from life. The woman, the career, the life; and Hoop … well, he hesitated. He always hesitated. It wasn't that he thought he didn't deserve to have it all, it was simply that he had lost so many times he'd sort of gotten used to losing.

And that was no way to live a life.

He had his career. He was confident and he knew how to go after what he wanted in the office and he was damned determined to make sure that he got the partnership he'd worked hard for … and the girl.

Damn.

He wasn't backing down on either.

This was his time and his moment and he had to own it.

Oh, damn. The infectious music was making him think of his life in broader terms than he'd ever contemplated before. He shook his head and realized that he was falling for this spell of believing that life was made up of everything he wanted.

He knew it could be.

"I'll meet you out front," he said to Cici and got up and left the theatre.

He was acting like he'd lost all his senses. He had always been pragmatic. Why did he suddenly think he didn't have to be that way?

Once he was in the lobby he stood to the side and saw a few other people doing the same thing. All on their phones. He could pretend he needed to check in with work but he didn't want to. He didn't want to try to build his future on lies and mistruths. His past had been built on fear and determination. Determination he was happy enough to claim but fear … it felt like a lie.

That he'd spent so much of his life trying to pretend he was okay and that he was well adjusted and then he talked to a guy like Nico who ran his family's yacht-making business and it hurt. It hurt more than he wanted it to. Because it reinforced how much he didn't know. That he had no heritage to pass onto his children.

Someone who hadn't been wanted from the first moment he drew breath and though he had fought hard to ensure that didn't define him, he knew deep down it did. Inside, he was still the baby no one wanted. The kid who'd bounced around foster homes for too long.

"Hoop, you okay?"

No. He wasn't okay. And he had the feeling he wasn't going to be *ok* for a very long time to come. Cici had changed him. Awoken things that he'd thought he buried so far and so deep inside of him that that he'd almost forgotten they were there.

But he wasn't about to tell her that.

He turned to see Cici standing there, looking sweet and sexy, the way she always did. But a part of him saw her as an avenging angel. As the woman who would hold his feet to the fire, no more pretending or faking it. With her he wanted to be the guy who he always hid from the world.

And tonight, when he had been her sounding board for her friend's new match, he didn't feel nearly as tall as he had before. He felt all those foster homes like an anchor around his neck.

He had a glimpse of a life he hadn't realized he wanted until he'd been this close to it. He wanted it badly. And sometimes when he held on too hard to someone, they disappeared from his life. It had taken him fourteen years to make it to the Fillions' door and even then he struggled to believe he was part of the family. Really part of it.

What if it took him that long to adjust to Cici? He couldn't ask her to just wait for him to figure his life out. To start to feel comfortable with her around. That would be ridiculous, but a part of him wondered if he'd ever truly feel like she was his. If he'd ever feel like she was in his life for the long haul.

Hours on the treadmill couldn't help him to process this. He had to accept the man he was and he had done a long time ago, but until tonight, until this moment, he hadn't realized that he was afraid to see what she thought. How she really viewed him.

"Yeah. Sorry, I just had to check in at work," he said. Lying. Damn. He'd thought he was going to be better than that. But the old doubts had worked their blackness on his soul and instead he answered with the answer she'd expect and take at face value.

"No problem. I needed to go to the bathroom so figured I'd check on you. I don't know that I'm ever going to get used to that part of being pregnant," she said and then laughed. "As if that's the hard part to adjust to."

"I think that's why you have nine months of pregnancy to help you come to terms with everything," he said teasingly.

"I think you might be right. I wonder if nine months is enough time?" she asked.

"Probably not," he said. Talking to her calmed him.

"Thank you."

"For?"

"Being in my life. Even though I was bratty about letting you back in," she said with a grin.

"You're very welcome," he replied, feeling strangely content.

They left Iona and Nico after dinner at a restaurant in Bryant Park. Cici hadn't wanted to take a cab so he was walking her home. The summer evening was balmy and a little humid but Hoop had a few beers at dinner and had a nice buzz going. He held her hand loosely in his and his mind was wandering, not focused on the stuff he knew the two of them would have to deal with soon.

"When I was a kid, before I came to live with my parents, I used to look at the night sky and think that someone was out there searching for me," he said. Damn. Where had that come from?

They were crossing through Central Park. Taking the long scenic route home and the sky had a little less light pollution here so maybe that was where that thought had come from. There were couples making out on the benches.

She tipped her head back and looked at the sky. He wondered what she saw up there. For all that she'd shared with him, there was still a big part of Cici that was a mystery. "Your parents were looking for you. And they found you."

He nodded. Lucky. He had forgotten how lucky he was. "You're right. It's hard to remember that the universe gives you exactly what you need, even if it doesn't look like what you want."

She arched one eyebrow as she looked over at him and touched her stomach. "I'm not in tune enough to figure out exactly what the universe thought I was asking for when it gave me this."

He laughed. She had softened lately when she acknowledged her pregnancy. Probably as she'd adjusted to it. Also, contacting Rich and finding some legal resolution to his involvement had to help. A part of him believed it was because she was getting more comfortable in her own skin. And with the baby that was growing inside of her.

"A wiser man than myself would have to tell you," Hoop said. "I'm sort of a Monday morning quarterback when it comes to life. Everything makes sense when I look back at it."

"Everything?"

"Well, not everything. But most things. I think … I think if you and I had gotten together that night at Olympus we would have been casual. Neither of us was ready for anything serious. So maybe this happened to force us to see each other in a different light."

"I like that," she said.

They walked in silence for a little while, her hand held loosely in his and then she pointed toward the sky.

"Do you see that? I used to think it was a star until I found out it was satellite. When I was a teenager, I used to think that it was my dad looking down on me. I was really struggling with things at home, the twins were in that rambunctious stage that some days I'm not sure they ever left, and sometimes I'd lay in the backyard and just look up at the sky and talk to that star as if it were my dad. I missed him even though I'd never known him," she admitted.

He stopped walking, pulling them to the side of the path so that they wouldn't block the way. "I miss the thought of my biological parents. Sometimes, when I do something that neither of my parents do or when I have a strong dislike to a scent or a food, I wonder if it came from one of them. One of those people who sired me and then left me behind."

She hugged him close to her. Wrapped her arms around him and made him feel like he wasn't alone. He hugged her back but

135

because he didn't want to look into her eyes and see pity or whatever else she might feel for him.

He was starting to believe that Cici was his trial by fire. Because with every other woman he'd dated he'd been the confident family lawyer who knew his stuff. The posh kid whose parents had a home in Montauk for summer holidays and a nice place in Queens where he'd been raised.

But Cici brought him back to basics. Something about her stripped away all the superficial stuff that he thought was the real man and revealed the stuff he'd ignored or pretended didn't exist for a long time.

He hated that.

Yet at the same time, he was addicted to it. A little bit of his past was like a tooth ache that he couldn't help touching with his tongue. He knew the pain was there but he kept poking at it any way.

"I'm sorry that you had to experience that, Hoop. I think that it made you the man you are today but I wish that your past had been easier."

He turned and they started walking again. "When you put it like that, I guess I wouldn't want things to be different. To be honest, I can't imagine another mom or dad other than mine. I just would like to know certain things about them. It's a big black empty void. And it's not that I would want a relationship with them, I just would like an idea of who they were and what led to my birth."

Cici crossed her arms over her chest and rubbed her hands up and down on her upper arms. "I worry about that with this baby. I mean, I'm going to have to explain everything that happened but how am I going to do that? It's one thing to have a conversation with an adult but as a child … that's when I know I should lay the ground work."

"You'll figure it out," he said.

"I will?" Cici asked. "I wish I had your confidence."

"You do have it. I believe that you are going to be a fabulous mom," Hoop said as they started down the final path that led to her apartment building on Central Park West.

"You do? Why? I think I've been haphazard at best with this baby so far," Cici admitted.

"The fact that you care about how you will tell the baby. The fact that you are already thinking about these things … that's what tells me the kind of mom you will be," he said.

Her apartment had changed in the last three months. It was a home now. She had settled in. It was designer perfect but lived in. Cultivated with Cici's own style and sense of panache. And he was as charmed by her living quarters as he was by her person.

He wanted to stay here. He wanted to move in, settle down and never leave. And he envied her child. She'd created an oasis in the middle of the city. A place where…

"Hoop?"

"Hmm?"

"Do you want to stay?" she asked carefully.

"I have to be at work early," he said. "But if you don't mind me leaving, then I'd love to stay."

"I don't mind at all," she said.

"Yes," he said. He didn't even have to think about it. He scooped her up into his arms and kissed her, knocking her glasses askew and she wrapped her arms around his shoulders as he carried her through the apartment to the curving staircase that led to her bedroom.

Up the sweeping stairs, he didn't have to worry about the anchor of the past or what the future held. He had the future. He had it right here in his arms.

He was tired of never feeling like he was enough. Like he wasn't good and should be grateful for every little thing he had. He was enough.

He was enough for Cici and her little bean.

And tonight had shown him that. He'd seen her friend on a blind date. Seen a man who wanted to impress and realized something fundamental that he'd never imagined before.

Everyone felt like they weren't enough.

He set Cici on her feet next to the bed, which had tons of pillows at the head and a brightly colored comforter with a floral design on it. The night stands each had a lamp on it and one of them had an old fashioned red display digital clock. No smart phone mount for Cici. She was a blend of everything solid that he loved from the past and then glimpses of the best tech from today.

"Are you okay tonight?" she asked.

"I am. Better than I thought I would be."

"Good. I … I've been thinking about something," she said, sitting down on the edge of the bed and then bending over to undo the buckle on her sandal and he squatted down in front of her to do it for her.

She brushed her hand through his hair as he stooped in front her of her and her touch, as always, soothed the savage part of him. The bad boy troublemaker that dwelled deep inside of him and always was one step away from setting the world on fire.

"What have you been thinking about?" he asked, taking her shoes over to her closet and setting them on the box she'd left out that morning. He toed off his shoes while he was there and put his belt and wallet on the valet table she'd left in her room for him.

She'd given him a spot in her house, he'd done the same for her, but his place felt like a place to crash and this … this felt like home.

"Do you want to move in here?"

"What?"

He wasn't sure he'd heard that correctly. He turned around, walked back to the bed and sat down next to her.

"Do you want to live with me?" she asked.

"Yes. More than anything. Are you sure?"

"Yes and no," she said with a little laugh. "I want you here with me but I have no idea what the next four months are going to be like. I think I'm going to be bigger and I don't want you to think for a moment that is why I'm asking you to live with me."

She would need help and he would have offered anyway. She meant something to him. More than he wanted to admit because then he might ruin this. "Why did you ask?"

"It was tonight as we sat together on that date. I realize … how much you mean to me. How much having you by my side is what I want. And I'd been hesitating to try to wait for everything to be perfect but life isn't perfect, is it?"

"No, it's not," he said, lifting her off the bed and onto his lap. He turned and laid her on the bed next to him and she looked up at him the way she did sometimes with hesitancy in her eyes.

"What is it?"

"I'm getting bigger now. My belly …"

He pushed her shirt up until he could see it. That tiny little bump that housed her little bean. The baby that he wished was his.

Damn.

He hadn't wanted to admit that even to himself but there it was. He leaned down and kissed her stomach and she put her hands in his hair holding him there. "I don't see anything objectionable."

"Oh, Hoop."

"Oh, Cici," he said back. Because really what else could he say. He wanted her. Not just in his arms tonight but he was beginning to believe that forever wouldn't be long enough and there was no way he was ever going to be able to just walk away from her or her baby.

Her hands on his head urged him to move up and he kissed her. Long and deep trying to convey what he was feeling but wasn't sure he'd ever be able to say out loud. He longed to make her a permanent part of his life. His instable, constantly in flux, always solo life. And he was afraid to reach out and try to hold her so instead he made love to her.

He took off all of their clothes and caressed every inch of her changing body and when he entered her their eyes met and Hoop felt something so deep and profound that he had to look away. After they had both been sated he rolled to his side and held her in his arms all night with only the thin blanket over them.

He told himself he couldn't sleep because even though he had spent the night in her bed before, this was different. This was going to be his home. *Their home.*

She stirred and curled herself against his side and he held her tighter. Looked down at her sleeping face and felt something well up inside of him. An emotion so deep and so powerful he was afraid to name. So instead he just whispered her name and held her closer to him.

Chapter 14

Hoop woke up early and made love to Cici before leaving her nestled in the rumpled bed, sleeping. He wanted to call in sick to work, the first time that had happened in a really long time.

But he didn't. He was going to have the rest of his life with Cici. He only felt a slight twinge of worry that he wouldn't as he left her apartment. He took a cab home to his, then packed a few essentials to bring to her place that night.

Hoop had three other meetings scheduled back-to-back and a deposition he had to take for the case he was working on. He wanted to get out of the office at a decent hour since he had plans with her so he ignored it.

The first two meetings ran long and when he finally stepped out of the fifteenth-floor meeting room, his colleague Lilia was waiting for him.

"Hoop, do you have a minute?" Lilia asked.

"Sure. What's up?"

"I'm not sure where to start," she began and then bit her lower lip. "I wanted to give you a head's up because you are friends with my client and referred her to me and I have the feeling Martin is going to get you involved in this."

"This concerns Cici?" he asked.

"Yes. The father of her child is already a client of the firm," she said.

"How did we not know that?" Hoop asked.

"We only had the name Rich Maguire but when I entered his address a file popped up and he's actually Richmond Maguire Hallifax III. Martin has handled his family for years. I wanted to discuss it, especially with him bringing you on board."

"He's already mentioned me to you?" Hoop probed further. Of course, he had. Martin had been brining Hoop onto all his cases to prove he was worthy of being junior partner. He'd have to excuse himself from this one. And things could get awkward.

"Thanks, Lilia," Hoop said.

"Do you have a few minutes to discuss this with me?" Lilia asked.

"Sure. Let's talk in my office." He walked down the hall with Lilia following him. Already trying to figure out how he was going to handle the situation with Martin.

"Martin's waiting for you in your office," Abby said.

"Thanks. Hold my calls," Hoop said.

"Obvs," Abby said with a wink.

He just shook his head and then he and Lilia entered his office, closing the door firmly behind him. Martin wasn't sitting in one of the guest chairs, instead he stood by the window that looked down on the busy city streets, staring out at the skyline. Hoop put his computer bag on his desk and then walked over to stand next to his boss.

"Good afternoon, sir."

"Hoop, sorry for dropping by unannounced. Oh, Lilia, I'm glad you are here as well," Martin said.

"Thanks," Lilia said.

"We have a delicate case that I'd like you to handle, Hoop. It's with one of our oldest clients. Lilia, I assume that's why you're here," Martin said.

Lilia looked uncomfortable and Hoop gestured for her to have a seat.

"I'm happy to get stuck into it, Martin," Hoop said. "But if it's the Johnson-Maguire paternity issue, you should know I'm dating Johnson. I had no idea that Rich Maguire was represented by our firm when I referred her to Lilia. I'm actually the one who suggested she get the papers together and have them signed."

The silence suddenly seemed louder in the room and Hoop wondered, if in this one case, he should have lied. But the truth seemed the only way to move forward with this situation. And he liked his job. He didn't want to do anything to place it in jeopardy.

"I would have done the same thing," Martin said. "You have been in the system so you know how important it is for legal matters with children to be formalized. There is just no other way to ensure that everyone behaves rationally otherwise," Martin said. "I think it would probably be in the best interest that I don't bring you in on this one. Which is too bad because the Hallifaxes are one of our longest standing clients."

"Is this going to be a problem?" Hoop asked.

"It's not unheard of for us to rep both parties but it's not the way I like for this firm to operate. Tell me about the woman," Martin said.

"She's a friend of a friend … I think it was one of those things where neither of them expected any consequences," Hoop said. He was not sure how much he should say to his boss. But this wasn't anything that Rich wouldn't have already told his family.

"Okay. Well that complicates matters. The Hallifaxes didn't know about the baby until the paperwork was filed here. I … I'm afraid I'm responsible for this newest wrinkle. I assumed we were representing Rich and phoned them. They want to meet the mother and they want access to their grandchild."

"He told her to get rid of the child and said he wanted nothing to do with it. She is moving forward as if this were her child alone," Lilia said. "She did ask me to reach out and see if he would be open to meeting the child if he or she wanted contact later."

"Good, sounds like she's sensible," Martin said.

Hoop wasn't sure how Cici was going to feel about meeting Rich's parents. He also didn't really want to be in this conversation about her and the strategy for the company.

"I think I shouldn't be involved in this any further," Hoop said.

"I agree," Lilia said.

"I'm sorry, Hoop, I just want to get the best result for everyone," Martin said. "Lilia and I will continue this discussion in my office."

As soon as they both left, Hoop went to his desk and picked up the phone.

He and Cici were just starting to build their own life. There was so much family tied to this unborn baby … and at a gut deep level he was happy for that child. Apparently, he'd had no family at all beyond the mother who'd left him in the hospital. No grandparents, no one else to care for him. But Cici's child had a lot of family.

He sat down in his office chair and didn't reach for his cell phone. If there was ever a time when he needed to make the call from his office phone it was this one. It was business and not personal. Yet how could anything with Cici ever be business? He glanced at his watch and knew she'd be in her office at the Candied Apple & Café, probably doing some new forecast for the classes that Hayley wanted to offer in the fall.

He dialed her number and listened to the phone ring. He held his breath when the line clicked and he thought it might be going to voicemail.

"The Candied Apple & Café, Cici speaking."

"Cici, it's Hoop. We need to talk," he said.

There were a few seconds of silence. "Did you see Rich's poster in Time Square this morning? Is that what this is about? I mean, I think him being in a blockbuster movie shouldn't make that much difference."

He turned on his desktop computer as his assistant poked her head around the corner of his open door.

"Coffee?" she mouthed.

"Vodka," he mouthed back.

She arched her eyebrows and then backed out of the doorway. Cici twirled the cord of the phone around her finger. She should have mentioned Rich being a famous actor last night but she had been enjoying the evening. For once, she'd felt like they might make it as a couple.

"No … what poster?"

"Well that TV show he mentioned he had shot has turned into a huge sensation. Apparently, he's the hottest up and comer in Hollywood and according to the article that Iona forwarded me last night, his show is on everyone's must-see list," she said. She wanted to bang her head on the desk but instead had a little acid reflux and reached for the bottle of Tums that was becoming her constant companion. "I guess that's probably why he didn't want to be involved in the kid's life.

"I hadn't heard that," Hoop said. "What's the name of the show?"

"I'll forward you the article," Cici said. "If it's not about his newly famous status, then what are you calling about?"

"Just wanted to give you a head's up about the legal case. And I'm calling simply as your boyfriend."

Something melted in her stomach and she felt flushed and warm. That was the exact reason she hadn't mentioned the poster last night.

"So, what is going on?"

"Our firm represents the Hallifax family, that's Rich's legal last name: Richmond Maguire Hallifax III, and when the paperwork went through our system a flag was raised and a notice sent to my boss who has been representing the Hallifax family for his entire career. He read the papers and contacted Rich's parents, assuming they already knew. And well, they didn't. And now they want to meet you and have contact with the child."

She dropped the phone as stars danced in front of her eyes. She swallowed as she felt that acid burning in the back of her throat and then turned, grabbing her trashcan in the nick of time and threw up into it. Through the ringing in her ears, she thought she heard Hoop's voice but she just put her head down and threw up again.

Rich's parents wanted to know her baby. She'd sort of hoped that the child would be able to make contact someday but she wasn't sure how she felt about meeting them now.

"Cici … oh my God. Are you okay?" Hayley said.

Cici looked up at her, her throat burned from throwing up. Her sight was blurry from the tears and as she saw Hay she just lost it. She tried to tell her what was going on, but all that emerged from her mouth was a stream of nonsense.

"No I'm not okay … Rich's parents … he's famous, the baby isn't just mine … what am I going to do?" she asked her friend.

Hayley knelt next to her chair, took the waste bin and set it aside before hugging Cici. "I don't know but you are not alone. I have your back. You know that."

Cici nodded.

She'd freaked but she was starting to calm down a little.

"Take some deep breaths," Hayley said gently.

Cici closed her eyes and tipped her head back, breathing deeply. "Okay. I … I need to brush my teeth. Oh, crap, Hoop!"

She reached for the phone, lifting it to her ear as Hayley opened up her middle desk drawer and got out her at-work toothbrush and toothpaste.

"Hoop?"

"Thank God. Are you okay?" he asked.

She heard the concern and panic in his voice and she felt a pang. He was a good guy. The best she'd ever had in her life and the last thing he deserved was the big ball of crazy she was bringing to the table.

"Yes. Sorry. It's the pregnancy hormones … well part of it was. The other part was straight up panic. Listen, can I call you back to discuss this? I assume there is something I need to do."

"There is. You have to decide if you want to meet the baby's grandparents. Lilia will be in touch with you."

"Okay. Thanks for this. I'm sorry you are caught in the middle," she said.

"I'm not in the middle. I am by your side," he said.

That solidness. The no fear in his voice slayed her. She didn't know what to say. A part of her realized that she wanted to cling to him. To let him be her support and tell her what to do next because she had no freaking idea what the hell she should do. She noticed that Hayley had left the office.

"Are you sure you still want to be there?" she asked. "I am not going to hold you to anything you said before this started. I mean, dating a pregnant woman was a big ask, but this … I'm not really sure *I* want to be in my life right now."

He didn't say anything for about thirty seconds but to be honest it felt like two years. "What kind of man do you think I am? Abandonment just doesn't sit right with me. I thought you knew me better than that."

Hoop left the office late. Cici had texted him after he'd hung up on her but the truth was he didn't want to talk. This baby had so many people that wanted it. But issues that he thought he'd dealt with, if not resolved then at least learned to live with, had raised their ugly heads once again. He'd been the baby no one wanted and Cici's child … well, it had grandparents and a mother and friends and aunts and uncles. It made Hoop go down the dark alley that led to the question of his biological parents. No one existed in a vacuum. Not in this life. So why hadn't there been anyone to claim him?

He had a great family now. The absolute best. On his lunch hour he went out to Central Park and walked. Listening to a playlist that his dad had set up on Spotify for him and his siblings. It was a summertime bunch of songs and as he walked and listened to it, his center returned. He no longer was in the dark place that Cici's comment had sent him to.

Only his dad would mix Kid Rock, The Eagles and Kayne West in a playlist. *His dad.* No matter who had been his biological father, there was no doubt in his mind that Pops was his father. He had influenced so much of the man that Hoop was today. He got back in the office and his assistant had a list of messages for him and handed him a package as he walked back to his desk.

"What's this?"

"I don't know," she said. "It was delivered by courier a few minutes ago. Martin wants to see you at 5:15. He said that you were aware of the topic and not to be late."

Hoop nodded. Martin hadn't stopped mentoring him just because of the case with Cici and the Hallifaxes. Something that Hoop was grateful for. He was trying to stay out of the case but he'd been copied in on Martin's email correspondence with the Hallifaxes. The protocol had been set up when he'd first started being mentored for junior partner.

He noticed that Martin was trying to get a decision from Lilia today. Hoop's gut said Cici might need more time to decide what to do.

The tactic of time pressure worked well to get results. He could see what Martin was doing. It was a technique that he had deployed himself in contentious divorce cases and custody battles. Family law was complicated because there was no way to stay objective for the parties involved. Something Martin was no doubt counting on with Cici.

"What's my afternoon looking like?"

"I moved Marlie Henderson to tomorrow so you have an hour free. What can I do to help with Martin this afternoon?"

"I'm not sure you can help. I'm waiting to hear back from the client to find out if the agreement is acceptable. I'm going to make a call and then do you mind seeing if Pete can take my 3pm? It's an initial consult."

"I'll see what I can do," she said.

He walked into his office and set the messages on his desk

as he held the package in his hand. It was a box wrapped in craft paper and tied with a piece of twine. His name had been scrawled on the top and he was sure it was Cici's handwriting, having seen her grocery list on the counter at her apartment the other day.

He undid the tie carefully and then took off the paper, using time to delay because he was unsure. He'd just found his center again and he needed to be lawyerly, not human. He needed to be bringing his A game and for some reason Cici wasn't inspiring him to do that. But then he opened the box and saw the card on the top.

He pulled it out, holding it loosely in his hand.

It was a piece of stationary that had her monogram on the top. He skimmed down to the note.

Hoop,

All my life I've been alone because I was afraid to let someone stand next to me. A part of me keeps hearing you say you will be with me but I don't want to trust. That's not fair to you. It's my fear, the same fear that led to the situation I'm in right now. I lash out when I'm scared and the way I feel about you is stronger than anything I've felt before. It scares me more than anything else. And while I know it's not fair to ask anything else from you, you've been great. Please know that I'm not really ready to say goodbye to you.

Cici

That she'd taken the time to write a note instead of texting or calling told him that she'd thought about it. Underneath her note was a box of Candied Apple & Café martini truffles. The ones that he always purchased when he stopped by to see her. She'd noticed his favorite.

He grabbed his cell phone and texted her.

Hoop: *Thanks for the note and the candy.*

Cici: *You're welcome. I'm sorry.*

Hoop: *It's okay. Do you need to talk about the case? I know Lilia is a great attorney but if you need any advice. I'm here.*

Cici: *I'm not sure yet. I haven't even spoken to Rich. He might not want his parents involved since he didn't want a kid.*

Hoop: *I'm here if you need me.*

Cici: *Thanks. Uh, I have a favor and it's okay to say no.*

He smiled.

Hoop: *What is it?*

Cici: *Lilia suggested I call Rich and I need to figure out what to say. Could you help me? I want to make sure he knows I didn't go to his parents and just want what's right for our baby. Lilia sent over some text but it's not me and I think Rich will know it.*

Hoop: *Of course. Do you want to come to my office?*

Cici: *Yes. I should be done here in thirty minutes. Would that work for you?*

Hoop: *Sure. See you then.*

Chapter 15

Cici took a cab to Hoop's office because the August heat was oppressive and she just didn't feel like walking. She'd been tempted to text her mom but a part of her, granted it was the rebel teenager inside, didn't want to get her mom involved until she'd sorted this problem out. She put her hand on her stomach and thought of her little bean who was causing all this trouble. Cici was going to be a mom soon. She knew she couldn't keep running to her own mother when things got tough.

She had to at least try to fix things first.

Then she was calling her mom and probably eating an entire pint of ice cream when she got home.

The cab pulled to a stop in front of the skyscraper that housed Hoop's law firm's offices. She paid the driver and hopped out and stood there on the sidewalk for a long time. Too long.

She wanted to run.

Again.

She wanted to just start walking, blend in with the crowd and disappear. Except she knew she wouldn't be happy living on the run or starting life over. It would solve one tiny part of her problem but then again it would open up so many more issues.

151

She was going to have to make up her mind about letting Rich's parents get to know her child.

But they wanted to know the baby. And she thought of her family … how she'd always had three sets of grandparents. Her dad's folks, Steve's folks and her mom's. She'd been lucky. And her little bean could be too.

She went inside the lobby and there was a reception desk to the left with two large security guards sitting behind it.

"Can I help you?" one of the guards asked.

"Yes, I'm here to see Jason Hooper," she said.

"I'll need your name and some form of picture ID," the guard said.

"Cici Johnson," she said, digging in her bag for her wallet and then struggling to get her ID out of the clear plastic slot. She handed it over to him.

He glanced at it and then entered her name in the computer. "Someone will be down to collect you in a moment."

He pulled a badge from the printer and handed it to her. "Put this on and then please have a seat."

He handed her ID back to her. She put the sticker on her shirt and then went to sit down. Her mouth felt dry and she fumbled in her bag for her water bottle. She took a long swallow and then a deep breath as she put the bottle back in her bag. She had nothing to worry about.

Hoop was on her side and together they would be able to fix this. She tipped her head back and closed her eyes, trying to still the worry that was circling around her. It was one thing for her to have doubts about herself as a mom; it was entirely different to think that Rich's parents might meet her and think she wasn't suitable to raise her child. Not that anyone had suggested that was why they wanted to meet her, but she thought it could be.

Once she opened the worry floodgate a million different things started to swirl in her mind. All the things she wasn't good at.

"Cici Johnson?"

Cici opened her eyes to see a woman in her late twenties wearing a slim fitting shirt dress. She had long, straight brown hair and wore a pair of heavy rimmed glasses.

"Yes," she said, standing up.

"I'm Abby Stephens, Jason's assistant," Abby said, holding her hand out to Cici.

Cici shook the other woman's hand. "Nice to meet you."

"You too," Abby said. "Let's go up to Jason's office."

Abby made small talk about the weather and the Yankees as they took the elevator up to the fifteenth floor. And Cici did her best to respond but she wasn't really in the right head space for small talk. She wanted this meeting to be over so she could just go home and hide from the world.

She couldn't help feeling a little resentful that she had to deal with all of this stuff since Rich had opted out of her life. Things would have been different if he'd been more open to the baby and to some sort of co-parenting. But he hadn't been and Cici was thinking that if he had a hot new show and the article Iona had sent her mentioned a fiancée, then the last thing he was going to want was a baby from some one night stand.

She rubbed the back of her neck as they stepped off the elevator. "Are you okay?"

"Yeah," Cici said. "Just hot."

"Come on, let's get you seated and I'll get some ice water for you."

"Thanks," Cici said, following Abby into an office.

"Go on into Jason's office, I'll be in with the water in a minute," Abby said, gesturing to another doorway with the door halfway open.

Cici walked over and hesitated on the threshold, glancing in to find Hoop sitting at the conference table with a lot of files and books in front of him. Lilia was there as well.

"Hoop."

"Cici," he said, glancing up at her. "Come on in."

She walked over to the table and he stood to hold a chair out for her. She sat down and then felt that same sense of panic that had overwhelmed her when he'd called earlier. But Hoop put his hand on her shoulder and squeezed and she felt a sense … well, not of calmness exactly, but of something a little less like panic wash over her.

Lilia's phone pinged and she glanced at the screen. "I've got to take this. Be right back."

"Where's Abby?" Hoop asked after Lilia had left.

"Getting me something cool to drink."

"Okay, while she is doing that, I want you to read over this," Hoop said, handing her a piece of paper.

"Thanks for doing this," she said, looking up at him.

"Not a big deal. I want you to get the results you want," Hoop said.

Hoop was good at his job. Nine times out of ten, he usually was able to come to a settlement in his client's favor and most of the time it was amenable to the other party as well. But this … well this was different.

He had no idea what Rich was going to say when she talked to him on the phone and he was really hoping that if Cici read the script he'd drafted, that perhaps Rich would side with her. Convince his parents to allow Cici to set the terms of the visitation.

"I don't think I'd say *acquiesced to your wishes*," Cici said. "I'm not even sure what that really means. I mean I can sort of figure it out but I wouldn't say that. This is really much nicer than I'm feeling about Rich at the moment."

"I get that. And the conversation can go however you want it to go. Just remember that if you're calm and sound reasonable, he will most likely react the same way. If you get emotional … I think that will be his cue to react. You want him to remember that you were honoring his wishes when he said he wanted nothing to do with the child. That issue should remain between the two of you. And that he has already given you a written statement that he didn't want the child and if you proceeded with the pregnancy he would have nothing to do with it. The legal paperwork was just a formality since he'd already expressed himself in writing to you."

Cici smiled over at him. "Damn. I think I better be careful what I text you in the future."

He winked at her. "I'm a lawyer first so I always think in these terms. And I want Rich to remember that the only thing that has changed is his parents knowing the two of you hooked up."

"That sounds …"

"Harsh? I don't mean it that way, I'm not judging. It's just that you need to keep to the facts when he is on the phone. Don't give him an opening or he might flounder and all of a sudden want things he gave up." Like maybe Rich would want Cici back. And he knew it was better for a child to be raised with both parents. So he'd have to do the right thing … back out of their lives, even though he had just started to feel like Cici was his. He thought about the suitcase tucked in the corner of the office that he'd been planning to bring to her apartment that evening.

"You don't want me to meet with them, do you?" Cici asked.

He stood up and walked over to the inner office door and closed it, leaning back against it.

"I do want you to. The more I see of Rich on paper, the more he seems like the kind of a guy who would make the perfect father for your baby. The bean would have a large extended family and you would have a support network of relatives there for you. A family with heritage … he's a III. I'm a … 'he looks like a Jason' … that's how I got my name. A nurse thought I looked like a Jason. I have no legacy, no heritage …"

"Stop it," she said, coming over to him.

She put her hand in the center of his chest and looked up at him.

"Rich was the guy who said it was one night, don't try to make it more. And you have a family, parents, a sister, a brother, Garrett who I know considers you like a brother, Garrett's family."

Hoop put his hand over hers. "I know that. I wasn't taking anything from them. But I don't know where I come from."

"I don't think it's very great knowing where Rich comes from. That attitude of his has to come from someone. What if his parents are like that?"

Hoop didn't think they would be. But he understood what she was saying. He tugged her off balance and into his arms. It felt like it had been forever since he'd held her and he was tired of talking and thinking.

He leaned down and kissed her long and deep and for a moment the buzzing in his head stopped. For a moment it was just Cici and him and that was perfect. He lifted his head, noticing that her skin was flushed and her lips were a little swollen from his kiss.

She arched her eyebrows at him and then stepped back.

"Let me open the door. Abby won't come in unless it's open," Hoop said. "Rewrite the script however you want. It was really just to give you a guide."

"Okay."

She went back to the table and he opened the door to find Abby on the phone. She looked up at him and held out a bottle of water and a glass embossed with the firm's logo. He took it from her.

And then he went back into his office. Cici was bent over the paper, writing, and he stood there just watching her and feeling that sense of not wanting to lose her. Not wanting to screw this up. He always felt the closer he got to something or someone he really wanted, the harder it was to remain distanced from them.

This job mattered before Martin had mentioned he was in the running for junior partner. He liked helping families come together and stay together. And a part of him knew that what he felt for Cici was important and deep. And if she had a chance to have it all … well he wouldn't stand in her way. He'd do everything he could to make sure she had the family of her dreams.

Cici was tense as she left Hoop's office and went down the hall to the conference room where Lilia waited for her. Hoop had already explained that there would be a paralegal in there who would take notes as they had their conversation. He'd also warned her that the notes would be sent to the Hallifaxes' lawyer as well.

"As soon as Mr. Maguire Hallifax answers the call I will introduce myself," Lilia said. "I will let him know we are recording the call and then transition to you."

Cici tucked a strand of hair behind her ear. "Okay."

"Ready?"

"Yes," Cici said, taking a breath.

"I'm ready too," the paralegal said.

Lilia put the phone on speaker mode and dialed the number that Rich had provided. The one she'd been texting him on. It felt weird to be calling him. But he answered on the second ring.

"This is Rich."

Cici felt her stomach drop. This was the first time she'd heard his voice since that night they'd slept together. And to be honest, she didn't really remember him sounding like this. His voice was deeper than she remembered and he sounded tired.

"Rich, hello, this is Lilia Small from Reynolds, Tanner and Crosgrove. We haven't had a chance to speak before but I am calling about the paternity issue."

"Damn, man, I told my parents I'm not going to pursue it," Rich said.

And Cici felt a sense of relief roll over her and almost started to speak but Lilia held her finger up.

"Don't say anything else, Mr. Maguire. I'm representing Cici Johnson, not your parents, and we were calling you to discuss

157

them. Are you still willing to talk to us?" Lilia asked. "I am recording this conversation."

"Crap," Rich said. "I thought you worked for Martin."

"Our firm is representing both parties in this case," Lilia said. "Are you still willing to talk to myself and Ms. Johnson."

"Okay. Well, I already told my parents what I told Cici, Ms. Johnson. I have a fiancée. I don't think she's going to be too thrilled to learn I hooked up while I was in Jamaica and got a girl pregnant."

Cici felt her skin heat up and knew she was turning six shades of red at least. She glanced at the paralegal who just kept her head down, making notes on the legal pad in front of her. Cici felt small and inconsequential as she listened to Rich on the phone. This was the kind of man that he truly was. Someone who was used to discussing intimate details with a lawyer. That wasn't something she was ever going to get used to. Before she'd heard him on the phone she'd been contemplating letting his parents perhaps be a part of the baby's life but now … she didn't feel as willing now.

Just a girl he got pregnant.

Those words echoed in her mind. Hearing him again just made her regret that she'd slept with him. She was embarrassed and realized she didn't need to be here for this conversation. She pushed her chair back, scooped up her purse and turned to walk out of the conference room.

"I can understand that," Lilia said as she left.

She hoped she'd understand that she couldn't have sat there for another second. She walked down the hall, realizing that she needed to get away. She took the elevator down to the lobby and then walked outside of the building. She felt like she could breathe for the first time when she stepped out into the hot, humid, June day. She switched her glasses for her sunglasses and went to stand against the building. Just breathing and trying to figure out what she was going to do. She knew that Lilia would get whatever she needed from Rich and for right now she couldn't do anything else.

Her phone pinged and she pulled it out of her purse, glancing at the screen.

Hoop: *You okay?*

Cici: *Yes. Just needed to get out of there. I'm going back to the store. Text me later.*

Hoop. *I have a client coming up, but I have asked my assistant to put him off. Do you want to talk?*

Cici typed the word no but didn't hit send. She had taken the afternoon off from the office so she didn't need to go back.

Cici: *Sure. I'm going to walk around the block and look for a place to get ice cream.*

Hoop: *Go north one block and there is a really great gelateria. I'll meet you there.*

Cici: *Thanks.*

She put her phone away and headed in the direction that Hoop had sent her. She realized that she felt angry. And it was the first time since she'd been to the doctor and confirmed that she was pregnant that she'd been mad. She'd been scared and unsure and disappointed, but this was the first time she was full-on-ready-to-kick-something mad. She entered the gelateria and got in line. She looked around, noticing that the place was full of a mix of tourists and families. She observed the families as she waited for her turn to order and some of her anger melted away.

She wanted to deny Rich's parents the chance to know her child because he was a jerk and she wanted to hurt him. But as she watched an elderly couple with what she assumed was their grandchild, she wondered if Rich would even care that his parents were denied access. He was totally self-absorbed. That conversation had confirmed what she already had guessed.

Did she owe it to his parents to give them a chance?

She knew her mom and stepdad would be upset if one of the

twins' girlfriends got pregnant and tried to cut them out of the baby's life.

"Hey, lady, are you wanting something or what?" the guy behind the counter said, interrupting her thoughts.

"Yeah, mango in a cone please," she said. She moved down the line and realized that she needed more time.

Chapter 16

When Hoop got to the gelateria, Cici wasn't there. He walked a few feet away from the ice cream shop and saw her. She was standing against the side of the building, holding a cup of ice cream with her head against the wall.

He ran over to her, took the ice cream from her as it was dripping down her hand. "Are you going to eat this?"

She shook her head.

He tossed it in the nearby trash can.

"What happened?"

Her face was white, her hands were on the small of her back, her belly had been growing but he hadn't noticed until this moment. Usually he just saw Cici and the glow of her personality. But now she almost looked like her pregnancy was a burden.

He pulled her into his arms and she hesitated for a second before she wrapped her arms around him and he felt the burn of her tears against his chest.

"Babe, you're freaking me out here. Are you okay?" he asked.

She nodded and then shook her head. "I'm not okay."

He tipped her head back, pushed her sunglasses up on her head, and wiped away her tears with his thumbs.

"Did Rich say he wants to be a part of your life?" Hoop asked. "Is that it? Does he want to share custody?"

"No. He called me a girl he knocked up and it brought home to me the man he really is. I wanted the baby to have a way to know him someday but really … is that the kind of man I want my child to be in contact with?"

"Cici, I'm so sorry," he said. He rubbed his hands up and down her back.

"Me too. I just walked away and I know Lilia wants me to do something, she's texted me twice since I left, but I just can't. I have to think. I need to get past this anger and hurt and figure out what to do next."

"We can do this together," he said. "I'll help you."

"Hoop, no. I have to figure this out on my own," Cici said.

Could he give her space? That's what she was asking for, right? Was it just space or did she need more time?

"We can talk about it later. When I get home tonight," he said.

"I think we should wait on you moving in," Cici said.

"Uh, okay …"

He was worried about her and he didn't want to pile on to everything she was trying to deal with at this moment. But why was she shoving him out of her life now?

"I'm sorry. I'm just overwhelmed and I need to clear my head," Cici said. "Thanks for coming to find me just now."

"Of course, that's what friends are for."

"I just need some time," she said.

"I'll give it to you," he replied.

How many times in his life had he gotten his hopes up for something and then had it turn out like this? Too many to count or remember. He had known better. Except that he'd been lulled into thinking this was different. *She was different.* But when the chips were down, she wasn't turning to him. She turned away.

He hailed a cab and put her in it. "Call me."

She nodded.

He watched the cab drive away. He knew she'd had a rough day and part of him hoped she'd call and say she needed him. But the more realistic part of him knew she wouldn't.

He walked back to his office. Work. That was what he needed to focus on. Abby handed him a few messages. He met with his client and then skimmed his emails closer, pretending he wasn't waiting for a text from Cici.

In his emails was a transcript of Lilia's call to Rich Maguire and as he read it, his heart ached for her. Rich was like many of his clients. A man at a crossroads. Not ready for fatherhood. And he felt pretty strongly that his parents shouldn't be interfering in his life. And that was what Rich was focused on. His folks trying to make him do something he didn't want to do.

This was messed up.

He knew he shouldn't get involved. He was being copied in only for information purposes and because one day Martin hoped that Hoop would be representing the Hallifax family, so he needed to be in the loop.

But this was personal.

Hoop was in love with Cici.

That was why he was thinking more about her than this meeting with his boss. This meeting with the man who held all the power over his future. But there was no choice, Hoop thought. There was only Cici.

He suddenly needed to talk to his dad. He wanted ... well, reassurance, he realized.

He took out his phone and dialed his dad's number. Texting was fine usually but he needed to hear his pops' voice.

"Hoop, hey, son," his dad said as he answered the phone.

"Hey, Pops. You got a minute?"

"Always."

"Uh ... never mind ..."

"Go on, son."

But the words wouldn't come to him. How could he ask the

man who'd adopted him what was wrong with him? How could he say that he wasn't enough? Still, after all these years, he wasn't good enough.

"Can I come home this weekend?" he asked. Realizing that he needed to be with the people who'd given him a chance at the life he had today. He needed to be away from broken families that might be fixed and his job, which reminded him of how fragile they were. And mostly, he needed some distance between himself and Cici so he didn't end up at her place in the middle of the night begging her to take him in.

"You bet. I'm taking the lobster pots out and I could use a hand with the sails.

"Thanks, Pops."

"You're welcome, kid. Love you," his dad said.

"Love you too."

Cici told the cabby to take her to Penn Station … she knew what she needed. Her mom. She needed to be away from the city and the posters featuring Rich and advertising his hot new show. Away from the pressure from Hoop and her own indecisiveness about what to do next. And one thing the three-hour train ride to Sag Harbor and the Hamptons would do was give her a chance to think.

She knew she'd hurt Hoop and that hadn't been her intention at all, but she needed to figure out the mess she'd made before she got any deeper into things with him. She cared about him more than she wanted to admit. Last night she'd realized that she wanted him in her future, which was why she'd asked him to move in. But it had been too soon.

She should have waited.

She purchased a ticket and then texted her friends to say she needed a break and pretended it was pregnancy health related. Not pregnancy stress related as it actually was.

Iona: *Are you okay? Where are you going?*

Cici: *The Hamptons. I need to get away from the city.*

Hayley: *Want one of us to come with you?*

Cici: *You are so sweet but I've already bought my train ticket.*

Iona: *It's midweek but I will be there this weekend.*

Cici: *You will be?*

Hayley: *You missed Nico calling and inviting her to join him for sailing.*

Damn. She hated that she missed that. Iona was so intrigued by her matchmaker-found man.

Cici: *I want details.*

Iona: *There aren't any … except maybe I kissed him last night!*

Cici: *And?!*

Hayley: *She couldn't stop talking about it when she dropped by this afternoon … speaking of which, how did the lawyer meeting go?*

Cici: *Sucked. It's sort of why I'm escaping.*

Iona: *Do I know what is going on here?*

Cici: *Rich's parents want to have a relationship with the baby. Rich is still a major douche who wants nothing to do with it. And … I'm not sure but it felt like Hoop wanted me to just agree to whatever would make his boss happy.*

Hayley: *That sucks. I think a few days at the beach is just what you need.*

Iona: *Me too. Can you meet me on Saturday morning preyachting for breakfast?*

Hayley: *Can I tag along? I'd need a place to stay.*

Cici: *You can stay at my parents' place. There is room for Garrett and Lucy too.*

Iona: *This is shaping up to be a fun weekend! I'm not sure what is going to happen with Nico. :)*

Cici: *Whatever happens, we will be there for you. My train's here. Text more later.*

Cici dropped her phone in her bag and boarded the train, finding a seat near the window and putting in her headphones. She had to transfer at Jamaica but she had a little while to close her eyes and try to deal with whatever she felt about Hoop.

It was hard to define, since she wasn't sure she wanted to face her own emotions. But she needed him to be more than her lawyer. She needed him to be her man. And today ... well the job had definitely felt like it came first.

She transferred in Jamaica station and found a seat near the window again. She briefly debated texting Hoop, but she wasn't ready to talk to him yet. She had already texted her mom to say she was coming to the cottage and hadn't heard back from her but Cici had her own key and if her family weren't at the cottage that would be fine with her.

She needed time to think. She had no idea what kind of people Rich's parents were but the fact that they wanted to get to know their grandchild made her want to give this decision some serious thought.

She remembered her childhood. She'd spent a lot of time with her Nanny and Pop-pop—that was what she called her father's parents. Her Pops had said she was blessed to have six grandparents looking out for her. And she knew now that Steve had been right. She'd always felt very spoiled by all of them.

She touched her belly. At almost sixteen weeks it was starting to become real to her. The bean wasn't just that any more, it was her baby. She wished she could hold her child. She hadn't found out the sex because she hadn't been ready to when her doctor had offered the information. But now she wished she had. She had read in the pregnancy book that knowing at this time gave the mom the space to adjust, but at this point she wasn't sure how much more adjusting she'd be able to do.

She'd thought the physical changes would be the most daunting but as usual, with the entire maternity thing, she had been wrong. It was the emotions.

They were killing her. She realized that she was about to start crying and jerked her phone from her purse and accessed her music app. She found the one song that always cheered her up ...

it was cheesy and she hit the volume button on her headphones until it was at the max she could stand and then hit play.

Suddenly, *Pocket Full of Sunshine* was blaring in her ears and it took about three bars of music before her gloomy mood started to fade away. She knew she had to be careful or she'd belt out the song, which would draw weird looks from the strangers on the train.

Then she decided what the heck … everyone on the train was a stranger and she found herself humming along. As the music went on she felt better and she lowered the volume as the song switched to another of her favorites. She'd stumbled onto her comfort playlist. Songs from her childhood like Kenny Loggins *House at Pooh Corner* and Gladys Knight and the Pips *Midnight Train to Georgia*. Each of these songs had been one of her parents' favorites growing up. And hers.

Even Steve's.

That shook her for a moment. The man she'd always thought had treated her differently had shared his favorite songs, his favorite sport and a lot of his time with her. Though it had felt like she wasn't as loved, she realized that she had been loved in a different way. And a little bit like she had told Hoop about being chosen by his parents, she realized that Steve had chosen her for his daughter.

Hoop vacillated between calling Cici and just giving her space. He knew that the phone call had to have been hard for her. But dammit, when was she going to stop running. He thought, hell, had hoped that by now she would have realized that he was on her side.

Was he?

He knew that he'd debated forcing her answer to keep him in line for the promotion but that had quickly faded once he'd thought about it for a little while. Martin was shrewd and Hoop hoped to borrow that technique he'd used today in the future.

But not with the woman he wanted to have in his life. Not with someone who meant so much to him.

He emailed Martin to say that his family needed him for the weekend and could he take the rest of the day off. Martin agreed and Hoop left the office and headed toward the garage where he kept his car parked.

He needed to get Cici off his mind.

After reading the transcript and what Rich had said about Cici, Hoop realized how badly used Cici had been. She'd never really let on about it; she seemed to almost feel like it was okay because she'd been using him, but honestly the conversation with the other man had made him livid.

He would be cordial because that was what was needed to get the results that Cici wanted. But after that…

He reached for his cell phone a million times … okay, that was an exaggeration, but it felt like it was at least a million times. And finally, he just gave in and texted her.

Hoop: *Hey. Are you okay? I'm guessing you need space but I need to know that you are okay.*

There wasn't a reply and as he stared at his phone he wondered if he should have left well enough alone. But he wasn't a timid man. And letting the woman he cared so deeply for just disappear didn't feel right.

Finally, he saw those dancing dots that meant she was responding.

Cici: *Hey. I'm fine. Sorry for bailing on you but I had a panic attack and had to get out of the city. I'm going to the Hamptons for some time away. I figured it would make things easier for you with your boss if you said I was gone.*

Hoop: *I'm glad you're fine. It's okay. I wanted to escape too. Sorry that conversation with Rich was so … well, horrible. Also, I didn't mean to add to the pressure earlier.*

Cici: *You didn't. I need to just forget about this for the rest of the day.*

Hoop: *Fair enough.*

He hit send before he could type anything else, like how much he missed her now that he knew she wasn't in the city or how much he wished he could have protected her from hearing the things that Rich had said about her.

But he didn't.

Hoop: *Are we okay?*

Cici: *You are great. I'm the one who has to sort a few things out. I'm not saying goodbye. I'm just hitting the pause button.*

Hoop: *Pause? For how long?*

Cici: *A few days?*

A few days? He didn't need a few days to think about his relationship with Cici. He already knew what he wanted. Them living together. She'd given him a glimpse of what he could have and then snatched it away.

And he knew he needed to be sympathetic. That she was pregnant and going through a tough situation with Rich. But he wanted, just once, to get what he wanted. Just once to have the family he'd always secretly needed but had always been afraid to claim.

Hoop: *Text if you need me.*

Cici: *Thanks.*

He stared at the smiley face emoji and wondered if she was really okay with him or if it were her way of just getting him to stop texting and he realized he needed a boys' night out before he headed out to the Hamptons. He needed to be with his friends and not think about Cici. He group texted Garrett and his old cop buddies to see if anyone was available for a night of clubbing and he got back a group of replies in a short time that said *yes* and *hell, yes.* He wanted to believe that blowing off steam was going to solve the nagging feeling in his gut but he was too shrewd to really believe it.

Chapter 17

Watermelon iced smoothies and long beach walks had started to define Cici's life. She hadn't talked to Hoop since their text exchange yesterday. And she was okay with that. She needed a break. Her mom had come to the cottage to meet her and it had been just the two of them. Her mom had been talking a lot about her pregnancy with Cici and about Cici's father; something that had really helped Cici to find her center again.

She knew she was running from Hoop and hiding because it hadn't been just Rich that had upset her. It was the fact that Hoop might think of her in the same light and that would break her heart. Right now, she needed to be pampered and no one did that like her mom. The cottage they owned in the Hamptons had always been a retreat from real life when Cici was growing up and it was no different now. Her brothers were all coming home and maybe it was the baby and the pregnancy hormones but for the first time she realized that she might have been a barrier to her stepfather.

It was hard to admit it to herself after all these years but as she watched Steve talking with her brother, she realized he never really treated her any different than he did the boys. Maybe it had just been her own feelings of inadequacy ... which made her think of Hoop, who'd grown up first in the foster system and then in an adoptive family. He was better adjusted than she was. How had he done that?

She missed Hoop.

It was silly to admit that even to herself, since she'd been the one to ask for space but she did miss him. There was no denying it. She'd gotten a few texts from Hayley and one from Iona, both of them checking up on her to make sure nothing was wrong. She'd ducked out on them too.

It was hard being friends with women who were so together. Who seemingly never put a foot wrong. While she knew the reality that they all did make mistakes, right now it felt like Cici was the only one making a huge mess of everything with each move she made.

She looked down at the fried chicken on her plate. It was oozing with calories and the old Cici, pre-preggo-Cici, would have sneered at the amount of fat and carbs on that plate, but now she didn't. In fact, her mouth watered as she lifted it up and took a huge bite. Delicious … if only everything in life was as easy as fried chicken, she thought.

Her phone pinged and she glanced down and choked on the bite in her mouth. She finished chewing and swallowing, taking a huge sip of her bottled water before she glanced down at the screen again.

It had gone black and she admitted to herself she must have been hallucinating. There was no way that Rich had just texted her. He was in Hollywood with his career blowing up and doing his thing. Why the heck would he be texting her? Especially after he pretty much said *I'm not interested in the baby or her.*

She wiped her hands and then picked up her phone. As soon as she pushed the unlock button the message popped up again and she almost dropped her phone as the preview of the message sank in.

Twitter DM from Rich: *We need to talk about the baby and about the future…*

The bit of chicken that she'd just swallowed threatened to come back up and the secrets she'd been holding for too long were ready to come out, she thought. She stared at the screen and realized that running away hadn't been her smartest idea. She needed her girls. She needed her support system. She wanted … hell, she wanted *Hoop*. She wanted to talk to him and hear his calm voice telling her that everything would be okay and giving her the sanguine advice that he always did.

But she'd run.

She'd shut him out and she really wasn't too sure that letting him in was a good idea. It felt a little bit like she wanted him to fix this for her. She wanted someone to fix this for her.

But there wasn't anyone else who could make this situation livable, save herself. She knew it.

She clicked on his message. He wanted to talk and had left her his agent's number. She shook her head.

She opened the group chat she had with Iona and Hayley.

Cici: *FML I think that I am in trouble. Rich just contacted me and told me to get in touch via a third party.*

Hayley: *Why isn't he going through the law firm? And why is he telling you to contact him via someone else.*

Iona: *That's a dick move.*

Cici: *Yes, it was. But I think he's scared … or at least I want to give him the benefit of the doubt.*

Hayley: *Do you want us to come out there right now? Or are you coming back to the city?*

Iona: *I'm betting no to the city. She's trying to avoid Hoop.*

Cici: *All true. I just need to figure out what to say to him. I mean, I want to ignore it but I'm not sure if that's the best idea.*

Hayley: *Garrett is working all weekend. I just texted Dad's driver to come and get me. Iona, are you in?*

Iona: *Yes. I'm at the shop. Pick me up there?*

Hayley: *Yes.*

Cici: *You guys don't have to come.*

173

Iona: *Yes, we do. That's what friends are for. We'll be there in a couple of hours.*

Cici felt tears burn her eyes. It wasn't that she didn't know her friends had her back, it was just that she had been so difficult lately, keeping everyone at arm's length, that she'd thought maybe they'd taken her up on her demand to be left alone. It was reassuring that they hadn't.

She tucked her phone into her pocket and then realized that her friends weren't the only ones who had promised to be there for her. Hoop had as well. She wanted to pretend that she needed his legal advice, which she totally did, but she knew the real reason she wanted to contact him was that she missed him like crazy and he made her feel like the woman she'd always wanted to be. One who was strong enough to face anything that was put in her path.

Hoop woke up on his yacht, The Lazy Sunday, wearing yesterday's clothes and one shoe. He rolled over and groaned as the sun hit his face; his head started pounding louder than *The White Stripes*. He folded his arm over his face and tried to breathe through his mouth to calm his stomach.

"Food?"

He groaned again. "Not yet."

He rolled over, burying his face under the extra pillow on the bed.

"Soon, because you have work and I have a meeting with the captain in two hours."

"Go away, Garrett."

His friend laughed and then Hoop heard the very loud sound of Garrett walking away. Why was he walking so loudly? He'd thought they were friends … hell, best friends, but this morning he was finding that hard to believe. He was in pain and for the life of him couldn't remember what had gone on last night. Drinking, to be sure. A few rounds of poker with the guys and then … did they take the boat out?

He forced himself out of bed because Garrett had a point. He needed to be at work today, he had a lot of paperwork to complete, and then … what?

He loved her.

Sure, he hadn't told her yet but he knew he did and she'd skulked out of the City like he was someone to be avoided, instead of the man she'd said she wanted to date.

He stumbled to the bathroom and took a very quick shower, which involved him leaning his forehead against the wall while he washed. He wrapped a towel around his waist and then headed to the galley where there was a greasy bacon and egg sandwich on thick toast waiting. Garrett and Xavier, another cop friend of Hoop's, were both sitting at the table, looking slightly more chipper than Hoop felt and eating in comfortable silence.

Hoop sat down gingerly across from them and started eating. "What happened after poker?"

"You wanted to show us the yacht," Xavier said. "But we stopped at the bar at the end of the pier first and drank and played pool. You bet Dev that you couldn't be beaten and then ended up losing."

"What did I lose?" Hoop asked, fumbling around in the drawer behind him where he kept his spare sunglasses.

"Your shoe. You bet him one shoe. For some reason this made sense to all of us last night," Garrett said.

Hoop shook his head. "Where is Dev?"

"After beating you he took a victory lap around the bar and met someone and went home with her," Xavier said.

"Wow. That was some night," Hoop said. "Thanks, guys."

"No problem," Garrett said. "Hayley went to Long Island and I'm not as big a fan of staying home alone as I used to be."

"And I'm divorced," Xavier said. "So, I needed a distraction. The ex and her new boyfriend took my kids to Orlando for the week."

Hoop reached over and patted Xavier on the shoulder. That

175

could be him if he kept on with this relationship with Cici. She was a runner. He'd hoped he could convince her he was worth the gamble but life had taught him that the harder he held onto someone, the more easily they slipped from his grasp.

He rubbed his head and stopped eating.

When had he fallen back into these old thought patterns?

Cici.

It all came back to her. Time and again she was the one who was making his life … change. He hadn't gotten this drunk in … well, he couldn't remember the last time.

"You okay?" Xavier asked.

Hoop nodded. No sense in trying to explain to his friend something he wasn't sure he understood himself. "Thanks. His phone alarm went off and he pulled it from his pocket and glanced at it. His Pops. He was supposed to be helping him with the lobster pots today.

"Damn. I've got to go," he said getting to his feet. He threw away the last half of his sandwich and washed the plate, leaving it on the drainer. "Just leave your dishes in the sink, I'll have the cleaning service send someone down later. Could you lock up when you go?"

"No problem," Garrett said.

"Actually, I have to go now," Xavier said, as he put his dish in the sink and headed up the gangway to the deck and left.

"Me too. I wanted to ask if you were heading out to Montauk this weekend? Maybe I could catch a ride with you. Hayley has a car to bring us back and driving two is kind of silly," Garrett said.

"I'm heading there now. I told my Pops I'd be there this morning. I mean, I think that Cici wants some space …"

"You need to be with your family too, Hoop. Go and see your folks," Garrett said.

"Did I tell you anything last night?"

"Everything," Garrett said. "About the potential junior partner, how Cici's paternity waiver is adding complications, how you feel about her."

"Crap. I didn't mean …"

"You needed to. I've never seen you so … not like yourself. And the last thing I want to do is talk about my feelings or hear about yours, but this is affecting your job and I know how much that means to you."

"It does," Hoop said. "*Women.*"

"*Womon,*" Garrett agreed.

"Why is this so complicated? Did I tell you I'm the one who suggested the paternity waiver for Cici? So, all of this mess is my fault."

"It's not your fault. She hadn't thought through the complications of having a baby without the father involved and it sounds like Rich didn't either. They both just wanted to pretend it never happened."

"True. But the real world has intervened."

"You'll figure it out," Garrett said as they walked off the yacht and toward the cab stand. "You always do."

He wished he had Garrett's confidence but appreciated his friend's faith in him.

Cici stretched out on the lounge chair under the umbrella, pretending that laying on her back hadn't changed in the last few months. But it had. And she felt a little queasy. She rubbed her hand over her stomach.

"Bean, we are going to have to talk. I need vitamin D and laying in the sun has always been my favorite way to get it."

The nausea didn't subside, so she shifted around to her side, facing the chair where Iona was laying with her headphones in as she flipped through her magazine. It was one of those glossy, foodie magazines that had inspired the three of them to start the Candied Apple & Café.

Well magazines, Pinterest and Instagram, she thought with a grin.

"You okay?" Iona asked as she took off her headphones.

"Yes. Just can't lay on my back right now."

"Preggo stuff?"

She shrugged. To be fair, she didn't know if it was because of her pregnancy hormones or the fact that she was hiding out at her parents' house instead of facing the world. And the many things that were waiting for her.

"Maybe."

"Maybe? Aren't you sort of an expert by now?" Iona said, swinging her legs to the side of her chair as she sat up. She reached for her cover up and then her drink.

"Expert? Are you kidding? I'm pretty sure that the bean is going to be eighteen and I'm still not going to have figured out pregnancy."

Iona laughed and Cici smiled at her friend. She thought Iona was lighter somehow now that she'd given in to the pressure of her matchmaking mama. "Why are you so happy?"

"I'm not pregnant," Iona said with a wink.

Cici gave her a look though narrowed eyes. "I'm not unhappy because I'm pregnant."

"I didn't think you were unhappy about the baby at all. Are you?" Iona asked.

Iona was the first person to ask her that. And Cici realized that she honestly didn't know the answer. When she thought of the baby ... well, it felt to her like it was going to be them against the world. She'd have someone by her side that was hers. Not someone she had to share with another person since Rich was out of the picture.

But that had changed. One conference call had been like a bucket of cold water awakening her to the fact that she had never been as alone as she'd thought. There were so many other people who wanted to be a part of this child's life.

And at this moment, Cici was in charge of making decisions that would have lifelong ramifications.

"I don't know. I mean, at first, I was scared and whenever I think of actually having my child I am happy and a little anxious but the complications that are coming from getting pregnant by a man I'm not in a relationship with … that is something that is making me crazy."

"Making you crazy?" Hayley asked as she handed Cici a glass of ice cold lemonade. "I thought you already were."

She handed a glass to Iona and then sat down next to her.

"Ha ha. I'm being serious here. I thought it would be me and the bean and you guys and maybe my parents and brothers but now there are all these relations I am not sure I want to deal with."

Hayley tipped her head to the side, studying Cici. "You can say no."

"I get that. But what about when the bean is old enough to realize that her dad probably had parents and asks about them. And then I have to say I was selfish and told them they couldn't see her … I don't know why but I feel like the baby is a girl."

Hayley got up and came and sat next to her, hugging her close for a long moment and Cici hugged her friend back, resting her head on her shoulder. "I think it's a girl too. And it's not selfish to want to keep the baby to yourself. You started this thing alone. As soon as you knew you were pregnant Rich walked away and told you he wanted nothing to do with it. So, you have been setting things up in your head the only way you knew how."

"She's right," Iona said, reaching over to pat Cici's leg. "You did what you had to. Do you want to know Rich's parents?"

"No. But this baby might. I mean, I have a good relationship with my Dad's parents and with Steve's. Why should I cheat this baby out of the same thing?" Cici asked.

"Why should you? Because Rich isn't a dead war hero like your dad was and he sounds very selfish and not all that mature. What did you see in him anyway?" Hayley asked.

"He's cute and I'd had a lot of champagne and the man I really wanted had rejected me," Cici said. "It wasn't that hard to fall into his bed."

"Makes sense. I wasn't judging by the way, just thinking he's not your usual type."

"I know," Cici admitted. "I think that was part of the appeal. I was so tired of being me. I acted on impulse."

"Well, I have heard leap and the bridge will appear," Hayley said. "Like you had to do something to break the pattern."

"I certainly did that," Cici said. "But the guy …"

"You got Hoop's attention," Iona said. "And the baby is probably your bridge. It is your future. It was unfair of them to try to force you to decide about the other grandparents so quickly. I'm glad you came out here."

She looked at her friends and knew in her heart that she was blessed to have found these amazing women. "Me too."

"So, do you know what you are going to do?"

"I think so. But I'm going to let everyone sweat a bit longer."

Everyone except Hoop. But she didn't want to just text him and she was afraid that the longer she went without talking to him, he might realize he didn't need the complications she'd brought to his life. She needed to let him know *just* how much she needed him.

Chapter 18

Garrett was in a decidedly talkative mood as they drove out of the city. And Hoop regretted not taking his restored '69 Mustang convertible instead of the BWM. He'd tossed the keys to Garrett and let him drive because his head was still aching and he'd thought he could maybe sleep, but that wasn't happening.

"Then I was like we can't board Lucy, she's so small, and the other dogs might be mean to her," Garrett said, reaching into the backseat of the car and petting the miniature dachshund that he and Hayley owned. Technically, Lucy was Hayley's dog but Garrett doted on her like some men would their first child.

"Of course not," Hoop said. "Why are we talking about the dog?"

"So that I don't have to admit that I'm getting nervous about the wedding."

"What? Men don't get nervous," Hoop said.

"That's a lie and you know it. It's just that Hayley's dad invited me to join him at his club last week and he brought up grandkids and how he hoped at least one of them would follow in his and Hayley's footsteps … I don't even have kids and now I'm wondering if I am going to have to urge them to be the prince or princess of frozen meals … and my dad would probably love someone to follow in his footsteps … though Pete has that taken care of for right now."

"You're rambling."

"I know," Garrett said. "And now I've got the desk job and might be promoted to internal affairs, which would be nice, but then I'll be home more, which means I'm going to have to help Hayley with figuring out the kid thing."

Hoop started laughing. He couldn't help it. Cici was struggling on her own with the same issues. It was the circle of life. This was where people decided the kind of parents they would be. Not when the baby was born but in these months before birth or in Garrett's case, before conception. Hoop had been having these same conversations with himself since he started dating Cici and was no closer to an answer than Garrett was.

Garrett, who was engaged to the woman he was thinking of having kids with. He knew that Hayley had his back and still he was as confused as Hoop. It was oddly reassuring and it made him realize that maybe it was time to relax. Except relaxing had never really been in his nature. He was intense by design. Pops always said that and Hoop had never really disagreed with him.

"Laughing? Really? That's the kind of support I can count on from you?" Garrett said.

"Gar, you know I'm here for you, but your kid is probably going to be just like you. So, if you steer him or her away from the frozen food kingdom they will probably rebel and go for it and vice-versa. Or maybe one of them will have a passion for cooking the way Hayley does. You can't predict these things," Hoop said.

"You're right. I just want everything to be perfect. Hayley didn't have a great childhood and I want our marriage to make up for that," Garrett said.

He realized he wanted the same thing for Cici. But one person couldn't be responsible for that type of thing. He knew that. Logically, he felt it all the way to his soul, but he wanted to give it to her.

"So, you want to give her the world," Hoop said. "I think that's all you need to make things work."

"You think?" Garrett asked. "My dad said the same thing but you know how he is."

"How?"

"He thinks I'm panicking because of the wedding and that's why I'm freaking out a bit," Garrett said. "My brother is no help at all. He and Crystal are happy doing their own thing and keeping house with Baskins, their dog. But I know Hayley wants kids."

"How do you know that?" Hoop asked. For him and Cici, the baby was at the heart of their relationship and for the first time since they'd gotten together, he realized he resented that a little bit. He would have liked the time to get to know her without the pressure of knowing in five months she was going to have a child. And that would change everything.

"She talks about it all the time because of Cici. She's glad that she won't have to worry about the father like Cici does, and that she'll have me to lean on … and I'm all like, of course you will, but internally I'm like, we aren't ready for kids. Are we?"

For the first time, he had a glimpse into what might really be going on in Cici's head and it was coming secondhand through Garrett. But it made sense. She didn't want the world to know she was freaking out but of course she was. It was hard to deal with her body changing and the baby growing inside of her and then the paternity waiver and the grandparents she'd never met who wanted to be a part of her life.

And he was angry she'd skipped out on him. He didn't blame her, he got it, but it was hard to keep chasing after her when she just wouldn't stand still.

Until now.

Now he had a tiny glimpse into all the shit she was dealing with and he wanted to make it different, to have the courage he needed to just stand back and let her do what she needed. But he wasn't sure he could do it.

If this were some sort of perfect world, sure he could be the bigger man and give her space and time. But he wasn't the bigger man. He was scared and in love with someone who kept running. He was also more than a little bit afraid he was already connected to her child. He was going to lose everything if he couldn't figure out how to help her and reassure her.

But he didn't know how.

He was afraid he was never going to know how to deal with Cici. And the last time he gave her space, she ran and fell into bed with Rich. Space wasn't the answer. He texted his dad when they got to Sag Harbor and told him that he needed to try to make things right with Cici and he'd come to Montauk once he did that. His dad wished him luck and told him he looked forward to meeting Hoop's woman. And Hoop hoped that she would be his woman again.

"Hoop's here," Hayley said. She had come into Cici's bedroom with a glass of juice. She stood there in the doorway, all nervous and a little bit sunburned or maybe she was blushing.

"Why is he here?" Cici asked. "How does he know where my parents live? I told him they had a place in the Hamptons but wasn't specific about where we lived."

Hayley came into the room and flopped down on the end of the bed. Laying crosswise so that her feet dangled off the edge and her hair, which she had been letting grow, fanned out around her head.

"It's my fault. I invited Garrett to join me and he caught a ride with Hoop. His folks have a place in Montauk."

Of course, there was a rational explanation for it. And now she had to stop hiding. It had been nice while it lasted. But Rich had texted, and Hoop was here. It was time to stop skulking around and pretending that the world was made up of sand dunes, fried chicken and fresh fruit juices.

Her mom had gone back to Queens as soon as her friends had arrived so it was just the girls.

"Is he downstairs?" Cici asked.

"No, they are in town waiting to find out if it's okay if Hoop comes here …"

"Oh my God, Hayley, we sound like we're in high school."

"I know. It's this place. It makes me revert to all my crazy behavior when I was a teen."

Cici smiled as she looked over at her friend. "They can come here. In fact, I'm glad to see him."

"Promise?"

"Yes. You didn't do anything wrong," Cici said. She remembered something her mom had said to her a long time ago. About how true friendships were made, not in doing what was expected, but what was needed. And for most of her adult life she'd been lucky enough to not have to deal with too many crises. But the few times she had faced them it had been Hayley and Iona who'd rushed to her side and wrapped her in their arms and told her she was going to be okay.

So, there was no way she was going to wig out on Hayley. She was doing alright. The panic she'd felt in the law offices had subsided or at least retreated to a bearable level.

Hayley jumped up and ran over to her, wrapping her arms around Cici. "I'm sorry. I didn't think to ask who was bringing him. He just said he was catching a ride."

That seemed odd to Cici. Hayley and Garrett were in love and normally her friend was a stickler for details. "Why didn't you?"

She shrugged and walked to the window, which looked out over the backyard toward the beach. "He's been odd lately. Not like when he was debating whether or not to go back to being a cop, but I can definitely tell something's up. And then my dad took him to his club and I think … I don't know what happened. But since then he's … what if he's changed his mind? What if he no longer wants to marry me but he doesn't know how to say that?"

Cici went over to her friend, draping an arm around her shoulder. "That's not the case. He definitely loves you. And if he gets cold feet and bails on you, you will be fine. Iona and I and my little bean will be by your side."

"Thanks," Hayley said.

Cici hugged her friend and felt something shift deep inside of her. If Garrett and Hayley weren't sure of themselves how did Cici and Hoop ever have a chance? Hayley and Garrett were the perfect couple. They'd dealt with a lot of public stuff and made it through. In Cici's mind they were the gold standard by which she judged her own personal mess. She didn't want to see the cracks.

But now that she saw them she knew that it was significant. She tucked the thought away to examine later. Right now, she needed to cheer her friend up and get through seeing Hoop again. She was going to have to face him and she realized that she missed him.

A part of her had been excited, very excited to hear he was here. She'd run, and he'd followed. The pattern of their relationship once again exerted itself and she was more than a little relieved that he hadn't given up on her.

She didn't want him to.

It didn't matter that she wasn't sure what she truly wanted, she only knew that Hoop in her life was one thing that she needed.

"Text them and tell them to come … oh, ask if they will stop and get something for dinner."

"Like what?" Hayley asked.

"Fried …"

"Chicken again? You've had it for every meal since I've been here," her friend said with a laugh.

"It's the only thing I want," she said. "What a crazy craving. I'm going to stop eating it when I get back to the city. I swear."

Hayley sent the text and then she hurried out of the room to get ready to see her fiancé and Cici went into the bathroom to freshen up as well. She put on colored lip balm and tried to tame her crazy sun-bleached hair into something sleeker but she felt wild. She felt excited. In the pit of her stomach butterflies swarmed and she knew it was because Hoop was here.

Since the night when she'd first kissed him he'd been cautious and with good reason. She could acknowledge that now but the bond that had been forged between the two of them was stronger than before and there was no denying it; she missed him, she couldn't wait to see him.

She … loved him.

Jack Johnson sang about making banana pancakes and Hoop tried to relax. Afternoon had faded into evening and they were sitting around a bonfire on the beach, the evening had a chill but wasn't cool. Iona and her Greek date were walking along the beach, Hoop was sitting on an Adirondack chair that he and Garrett had carried down to the shore for the evening. And Cici was sitting on his lap, her head on his shoulder and she delicately ate a piece of fried chicken that he'd just gone and picked up for her.

It had been a fun day but it felt like pretend. They hadn't had a chance to talk. Just hung out with her friends and acted like they were anyone else taking a late summer weekend in the Hamptons.

At this moment he had everything he'd ever wanted right here. His best friend was talking quietly with his fiancée and the woman that Hoop loved was in his arms. A sense of rightness and peace spread through him and he realized how long he'd been chasing this moment. How long he'd been waiting for this feeling. He'd been afraid he'd never find it and of course it hadn't come when he'd been looking.

He would have sworn that he and Cici were perfect in the city but it was here in the dark with only the light of the fire and the full moon overhead that he'd found it. He snaked his arm around her waist and stole a piece of chicken from her bowl.

She swatted half-heartedly at his hand as he popped it in his mouth. "So … fried chicken."

187

"Yeah, I know. It's odd because normally I'm sort of not a huge fan of anything fried but this summer I just can't get enough of it. Mom said she craved burritos when she was pregnant with me."

"Burritos?" he asked.

"Yeah. They were stationed in Texas at the time. She said there was this restaurant she loved in College Station that made the best burritos she and Sheila, that's Mom's best friend, had ever had. They used to drive to get them at like two in the morning."

"Where was your dad?" he asked. He knew her father had been killed in action but he didn't know when that had happened or much about him.

"Deployed. Mom never said much about it before this. But I get the feeling that for much of her pregnancy he wasn't around. He was there the day I was born and he had one more tour to serve before he was out and ... he never made it back."

"I'm sorry."

"Don't be," she said. "It was a long time ago."

"It was a long time ago. But I know what it's like to never know your father. You must wonder about things, like traits you have that might be his."

"I do. But Mom was always good about including them. Making me feel like I knew him. She'd say, you're good at math like your dad or you eat Oreos the way he does."

"Cream filling first?" he asked.

"No. Intact and I don't dunk. I'm not a fan of a soggy cookie," she elaborated. "What about you?"

"I dunk after I've eaten the cream filling," he said.

"Gross," she said. "It's a good thing I like the way you kiss or you'd be outta here."

He tightened his arms around her and shifted her around on his lap until they were both facing each other. "You like the way I kiss?"

She arched one eyebrow at him. "Well I'm not keeping company with you because of your cookie-eating habits."

She was in a playful mood and he had to admit he liked it; liked this side of her. He wondered if she'd finally made a decision regarding Rich. And then pushed that out of his mind. He was here as her boyfriend and apparently as a great kisser, not a lawyer.

"What else do you like about me?"

"That's it, just your kisses," she said, with a wink.

"I'm wounded. I like tons of stuff about you," he said.

"Like?"

"The way you eat cookies," he said with a wink. But he knew he liked a lot of things about her. "I wasn't too sure that coming here was a good idea."

"I know. That's on me. I should have … I know I shouldn't have just bolted the way I did but I needed to escape. I felt the walls closing in on me and I just needed time to think."

"I get that," he said. "I really do. I was pissed as hell but I do understand."

"Thanks. I'm sorry I keep running," she said. "I was afraid this time you weren't going to come after me."

He tipped her chin up and looked into her eyes. He wished he could read her expression, but he'd never been good at reading the expression of anyone save another attorney seated across the boardroom table from him. "You wanted me to?"

She chewed her bottom lip and he groaned. She was turning him on and he needed to pay attention to this conversation. It was important, he wanted to give it the attention it deserved but she was sitting on his lap and confessing to things that made him want to make love to her. To reassure himself that she was back in his arms for good.

"I didn't realize that until you showed up here," she admitted. "I care about you, Hoop, I don't want to hurt you again."

He nodded. "I'm used to fending for myself, Cici."

"That bothers me. I should be coddling you and protecting you and instead ..."

"You are pregnant and dealing with a situation that you never expected. Don't worry about me," he said. He didn't want her to think about all the losses in his life or how sometimes he felt a little too much like a loser for his own good. But holding her now he felt like he had it all.

"How about you stop running and we try facing things together?" he suggested.

"Do you mean that?"

"Of course, I do. Do I seem like the kind of man who says things he doesn't mean?"

She shook her head. "It was more for me than for you. I'm touched you haven't just said to hell with me."

His heart was racing and he wanted to tell her he loved her but he wasn't ready yet. Wasn't sure he ever would be. What if he said it and then she left?

So instead he kissed her long and slow until his pulse was racing and his blood was running heavier in his veins.

Chapter 19

Cici took her time in the shower when they'd come inside. Hayley and Garrett were in the downstairs guest bedroom and Hoop … Hoop was using the shower between her brothers' bedrooms. They had a Jack and Jill set up with a shared bath. Iona had skipped out on them. Cici wasn't sure what had happened but Iona had breezed back into the house by herself forty minutes ago and said she had an emergency back in the city.

Cici had tried talking to her then and she and Hayley had both tried texting in their group but Iona was on total radio silence. There was no sign of the Greek billionaire she'd been matched with. In the morning, Cici vowed to get some answers. But for tonight she was waiting.

She'd taken a long time in the bathroom and now was staring at herself in the mirror behind the door. She had a baby bump but only if she told someone she was pregnant. Objectively she was pretty sure she just looked fat. Such a great feeling.

She tossed her semi-dry hair over her shoulder and tried to strike a pose but her confidence had taken a hit when she'd realized how big she was getting. Granted, she'd get bigger and so far, her ankles hadn't started to swell but still she wanted to look better than she did.

She'd always taken a certain pride in how she looked. She wasn't a crazy exercise maniac but she maintained a nice size. If she put on a few pounds she dieted to get them right off but this was different. Way different.

What would Hoop think?

They were lovers but they'd been apart and she honestly felt like the last few days she'd really started ballooning. Maybe all those lobster rolls were playing their part. Tomorrow it was water and carrot sticks … and maybe just one piece of fried chicken.

"Ugh."

"You okay in there?" Hoop called.

Of course, he was back in the bedroom. She grabbed her sleeveless nightshirt and opened the door. He was reclining on a pile of pillows; he had ESPN on the television and an open book on his lap.

She stood there in the doorway just staring at him. He had a gorgeous chest. All nicely defined muscles and he'd picked up a little tan today when they'd been on the beach, not like herself who'd picked up a little sunburn. She felt … like she didn't belong here.

"I forgot to brush my teeth," she blurted out and then turned around and retreated into the bathroom.

She went to the sink but didn't look at her toothbrush, instead she stared into the mirror and realized now that she loved Hoop everything was different. It didn't matter that he wasn't any wiser to her feelings. They were there now. It was all she could think of when she saw him. She wanted things to be perfect. Things like this night. She'd run away and they were back together.

Tonight needed to be one in a million and instead she was on the verge of tears because she was pregnant. And fat looking, and tired and it wasn't his baby. She had no regrets about the child. That wasn't fair to the baby but for the first time she admitted to herself she wished her baby was Hoop's. Really Hoop's. Not the way he was willing to be a dad to her child. But that it was his child too.

She let her head fall forward and realized that falling in love hadn't made anything better. In fact, she was pretty damned sure that acknowledging her feelings for Hoop had made things more complicated.

Had made her…

His hand on her shoulder stopped her runaway thoughts. He just squeezed gently and then she felt him move behind her, wrapping his arm around her waist as he pushed her hair aside and kissed the back of her neck.

He didn't say anything at all which was exactly what she needed. He dropped nibbling kisses down her spine until he reached the barrier of the fabric of her nightshirt and then he moved back up. One hand held her waist, keeping her pressed tightly to him and she felt his erection rubbing against her buttocks. His other hand roamed up her body, cupping her breast as she leaned closer and he whispered into her ear.

His breath was hot and his words were erotic and tempting, sending chills of desire spreading down her body. She stood there and all the fears and the irrational worry that had overwhelmed her a moment before faded away. She tipped her head to the side, turning so she could see him. His gray-blue gaze was serious and so sweet she felt her heart melt.

No matter what she had to protect Hoop. He was the sweetest most wonderful man and she wanted to make sure that she never did anything to damage him.

He stretched and kissed her. She turned in his arms to deepen the kiss. His tongue tangling with hers as his hands skimmed her back and pulled her fully into his body again.

"Your breath is fine," he whispered against her lips before he pulled back to stare down at her.

She felt exposed but it didn't bother her as much as it had before he'd come into the bathroom.

"Good to know," she said, then yelped as he lifted her off her feet.

She wrapped her legs around his waist and her arms around his shoulders. She rested her forehead against his as she was overwhelmed by the emotion of the moment. This was Hoop. A part of her had been afraid of giving into the affection she'd first felt for him that night in the Olympus but now it seemed silly to pretend that he wasn't the man she wanted to call her own. Not just tonight but for the rest of her life.

She pulled away from him and walked to the bed. This wasn't perfect. It was odd how he'd felt like love would make everything okay but now he realized it couldn't.

Loving her might not be enough.

It was a lesson he'd learned many years ago with families but he'd always thought when he found a woman, the right woman, it would be different.

He couldn't help just watching her, her cheeks were red from the sun, her shoulders tanned and freckled and her hair was sun-bleached from her time here. It hadn't been that many days since he'd last seen her and held her in his arms but if felt as if a lifetime had passed. His heart ached.

He wanted to make love to her as if that would fix things. As if by taking her body with his he could forge a bond that would make it impossible for her to leave him again. But he knew that wasn't true.

He shook his head.

Sex, man. This is sex. Make it about the physical.

Except that it had never been just physical with Cici and he had the feeling it never would be. If it had been he wouldn't have stopped that night at the Olympus. Damn, he wished now he'd have followed his gut instead of his conscious. Boy had that backfired.

"Are you coming?" she asked. "Your breath is fine too."

She gave him a wink over her shoulder and he stopped hesitating. This was Cici. The woman he wanted more than his career. He walked into the bedroom and took her in his arms.

She smelled of fresh summer peaches and the sea. Like a dream that he was almost afraid he'd wake from and find himself alone. So, he forced himself to scoop her up and sat down on the bed, drawing her onto his lap. She wrapped her arms around his neck and pulled him close to her. He felt the brush of her breasts against his chest and then she tipped her head, angling her mouth to deepen the kiss. She shifted around until she straddled him.

She put her hands on his shoulders and looked down at him. The hem of her night dress had shifted and he felt her bare thighs against his and when he swept his hands down her back and up under the hem, he realized she was completely naked underneath her nightshirt. He cupped her butt in his hands and shifted her around until he could rub his erection against her center.

"Comfortable?" she asked.

"Getting there," he said with a deep throated growl. "When we were sitting on the beach by the fire, this is what I wanted to do."

"Me too," she said, leaning forward to brush kisses against his chest. Her mouth was hot and moist as she explored his chest first with soft, thorough kisses and then he felt the edge of her teeth as she nibbled at his pecs.

He tangled his hands in her hair and watched her through hooded eyes as she shifted back on his legs to move lower. Her tongue tracing the line of hair that narrowed down toward his groin. He hardened even more as she slowly licked her way back up his chest and her tongue darted out and brushed against his nipple. He arched into her touch, putting his hand on the back of her head so that she would continue caressing him.

He ran his finger down the furrow between her buttocks and drew her closer to him. She shifted in his arms, her hands coming to his shoulders as she rocked her pelvis against his. He felt his manhood straining against the fabric of his boxer briefs and reached between their bodies to free himself.

She moaned as she rocked herself along the edge of his erection. She reached between their bodies now, tracing each of the muscles that ribbed his abdomen and then slowly lower. He could feel his heartbeat in his erection and he knew he was going to lose it if he didn't take control.

But another part of him wanted to just sit back and let her have her way with him. When she had him in her hand, he was about to lose it, and she winked up at him.

"I guess you like that."

"Hell, yeah," he said, pulling her nightshirt up and over her head and then his hands fell to her breasts. They were fuller than the last time he'd touched them. Her nipples larger and as he stroked his finger over them they tightened. He put his arm along her back and the line of her spine, holding her upright as he moved forward to undulate his chest against her breasts. She bit her lip and closed her eyes as his chest brushed over her nipples.

"I like that," she said.

Blood roared in his ears. All he could think about was getting inside of her and staking his claim, showing her with his body that she was his. He reached for her thigh, caressing his way up the outside and then moving toward the center but it was too much. She was so soft. She moaned as he neared her center and then sighed and spread her legs a little as he brushed his fingertips over her feminine secrets.

He slipped one finger into her body and hesitated for a moment, looking into her eyes. This was his first time making love to a woman he loved as much as he did Cici. He wanted to watch every moment of this. To commit it so completely to his soul that he'd never forget any part of it.

She closed her eyes and he took a moment to just watch her as he added a second finger in her body and she shifted around, her muscles tightening around him as he moved them inside of

196

her. He found her clitoris with his thumb and touched it lightly. She squirmed against him.

He pulled her head down to his, tangling his fingers in her damp hair, tasting her passion and he thought maybe her affection. He wanted to believe that she was going to be able to feel how much she meant to him from this kiss. Her mouth opened over his, their tongues tangling together. He wanted to take it slow and savor this moment but he couldn't. Not with Cici.

He skimmed his gaze down her body, she was perfect. Her full breasts, the tiny baby bump. Her skin both creamy and lightly tanned. He fondled her, running his finger around the areole of her nipple, watching as it tightened even more. It was velvety compared to the satin smoothness of her breast. He brushed his finger back and forth until she bit her lower lip and shifted on his lap.

Her breasts seemed more sensitive than the last time he'd made love to her. He scrapped his fingernail over her nipple and she shivered in his arms. He pushed her back a little bit so he could see her. Her breasts were bare, nipples distended and begging for his mouth. He lowered his head and suckled as he kept his fingers thrusting inside of her.

He used the hand he had in her hair to tug her gently back until she was arched, her breasts thrust up at him. She leaned frantically into him, and he increased the pace of his fingers in her body. He lifted his head and blew on her nipple as he saw gooseflesh spread down her body.

He loved the way she reacted to his mouth on her breasts. He kept his attention on them. Her nipples were so sensitive he was pretty sure he could bring her to an orgasm just from touching her there.

But he needed to be inside of her, wanting to share this orgasm with her. He held her close. He was so hard he thought he'd die if he didn't get inside her.

He glanced at her and saw she was watching him. The fire in her eyes made his entire body tight with anticipation.

He held her hips steady and entered her slowly. Thrust upward until he was fully seated. Her eyes widened with each inch he gave her. She clutched at him, her nails digging into his shoulders.

He leaned up and caught one of her nipples in his teeth, scraping very gently. She started to tighten around him. Her hips moving faster, demanding more but he kept the pace slow, steady. Wanting to draw this out now that he was inside of her, except that she was having none of that. She buried her fingers in his hair, pulling his head away from her breasts and leaned down, biting his lower lip before thrusting her tongue into his mouth.

She rode him, faster and faster and he held onto her, letting her set the pace until he felt that tingling of sensation down his back. He reached between them, touching her until he heard her moan and then she started tightening around him, pulling her mouth from his and throwing her head back. He kept thrusting into her until his orgasm rocked through him.

She collapsed in his arms, her head on his shoulder, her hair draped along his chest. He felt her breath against his heart and he closed his eyes and held her gently because he wanted to wrap her in a bear hug and make sure she never left his side again. But he couldn't do that. She wasn't ready for that. And he knew that if he told her he loved her and she walked away that he was going to be not only a broken man but unsure if he'd have the strength to follow her again.

Chapter 20

Cici knew that something fundamental had changed between herself and Hoop last night and when she woke up and found the note from him that he'd gone out for a run, she stretched and smiled to herself. She texted Rich back, agreeing to meet with him later in the morning and then got dressed.

She put her hand on the baby bump and realized that she and the bean were going to be okay. More than okay. No matter what happened. She'd talk to Rich and then gauge what rights she should offer his parents. And her friends had been right yesterday when they'd said she already knew what she was going to do.

She'd thought she was so mature and grown up but these last few months being pregnant had taught her how little she actually had. Her hard fought and well-earned independence aside, she was coming to understand that parents needed a large support system. When she thought of her own childhood she realized how much richer it had been because of Dad and her brothers. And the six grandparents she'd been lucky enough to have. She knew that she wanted that for the bean. She needed her baby to have all the extended family.

And she wanted a father for this baby.

Not Rich. Never him. *But Hoop.* He'd come after her so many times and she knew that if she'd been afraid to trust, afraid that he'd stay, he'd given her his answer a hundred times over.

She went downstairs and made herself a cup of herbal tea after sniffing the can of coffee her parents kept in the cupboard. She missed coffee, but she wanted her baby to have every advantage so this wasn't really a huge sacrifice. It was in a small way to her, but she didn't mind it.

She heard someone on the stairs and turned to see Garrett standing there in a pair of khaki shorts and no shirt. His hair was rumpled and he looked sleepy.

"Morning," he said, rubbing his hand over his chest. "Sorry. I didn't hear anyone down here. I was hoping to bring Hayley back a cup of coffee before she woke up."

"Help yourself. I'm restricted to tea but I love the smell of coffee so I'm going to sit right here and breathe it in."

He gave a hearty laugh and then headed to the Keurig machine. "Hey, sorry for bringing Hoop. I didn't realize what an awkward position I would be putting you in."

"It's okay. Actually, I'm glad you did bring him. I am a little like a tortoise when it comes to relationships and I think you helped move us forward by weeks by doing it."

Garrett put the first cup of coffee on the counter and then turned to make a second cup. "Really? You strike me as somewhat impulsive."

"I am impulsive, which leads to the slowness because I don't think things through," she said.

"Makes sense," Garrett said, putting milk into one of the cups and then adding sugar.

She heard the jingling sound of Lucy's collar and charms and a moment later the little dog trotted into the kitchen. Garrett reached for the leash and poo-bag but Cici hopped up.

"Let me do it. You take Hayley her coffee."

"Thanks!" Garrett said, taking both of the mugs and leaving the kitchen.

Cici stooped to fasten the leash on Lucy and then stood and got a little dizzy. The little dog tugged on the lead but Cici took a few deep breaths until the dizzy spell passed and then she put on her flip-flops she'd left by the door and took the little dog outside.

Lucy started trotting toward the sidewalk and given that it was a nice morning, Cici thought a walk would be a good idea. She'd left her phone at the house but she didn't worry. She knew most of the permanent residents on the street and the vacation renters were usually the same people year after year.

She put her hand on her stomach as she walked the dog and thought of the life that the bean was going to have here. The consistency and the security of growing up in the same place that she had and something else shifted and settled inside of her.

Hoop had said that her pregnancy was nine months long to give her time to adjust and she was just starting to understand the adjustments. She thought it was the idea of having a baby but that was simply the tip of the iceberg. There were so many other parts of her life that she was going to have to get ready for this child.

Lucy did her business, but Cici wasn't ready to go back yet. They were already pretty close to the main street in the village and she remembered how much Hoop had liked the pastries she'd brought him on the yacht so she decided to pick up some for them for this morning.

She didn't have her wallet but the owners knew her and her parents and they had an account at the store. Not a lot of places still did that but it was one of the many things she liked about this small village. It was a community and it was her safe place. The one place where she felt like the rest of the world really didn't matter.

When she got home she was going to call her mom and thank her. She realized how much her parents had given her and how much she owed them.

She turned the corner onto Main and noticed someone who looked like Rich sitting in front of the café.

She wasn't ready to talk to him.

But maybe fate had put him in her path for a reason. The door to the café opened and then Hoop emerged with an older gentleman that bore a striking resemblance to Rich.

His dad?

She stood there for a minute trying to process what she was seeing. But all she could do was react with anger and hurt. It looked like Hoop was meeting with Rich and his parents. Why would he be doing that?

Hoop hadn't expected to see Martin in the village this morning. But when he had waved him over, he'd gone.

"Martin, I had no idea you were in the Hamptons this weekend."

"I am here with the Hallifaxes. They brought Rich out here and are trying to get a meeting with Cici Johnson. They want to talk to her."

"I'm not sure she's ready," Hoop said.

"Maybe we can help her to be?" Martin said.

"I'm not her attorney," Hoop reminded his boss.

"I know. But this is something that isn't going to get solved with lots of hard-nosed tactics. Help me get some resolution here."

He hoped that this would be an opportunity for Cici. But he regretted that decision almost as soon as he'd made it. He wasn't in a position to even guess at what Cici wanted except maybe more time, and he knew that they weren't going to give it to her because he had coffee with them.

He was trying to think of a polite way to say that when he came back out of the diner to the table where Rich was waiting with his parents. He glanced up and saw Cici standing at the corner. He went to her. There was no time to think about anything other than she looked upset and he didn't want her to think that he had gone behind her back to set this up.

As soon as she noticed him walking toward her, something changed in her expression. She glanced down at Lucy who had taken the opportunity to sit down since they weren't moving.

"Hey. Martin was waiting here when I jogged by and invited me for coffee."

She nodded.

"Martin insisted. He wanted me to understand that they weren't monsters."

He started to talk again but she held her hand up. "It's okay. Right now, I guess I should meet with them."

"Only if you want to. You're not prepared, which I think is why they tried to catch me out by myself," he said.

"How did they know you'd be here?" she asked.

"They didn't. They knew your folks had a house here. Apparently, they got it from your cousin."

He wasn't sure what was going on in Cici's mind. She seemed to have shut down completely. And he wanted to do something to help her but he felt powerless. He could only offer his support. "Do you need me as a lawyer or your boyfriend right now?"

She looked up at him and nibbled on her bottom lip. "Both, I think. Let's go and talk to them."

As soon as she said, 'let's go' Lucy stood up, but Hoop's gut told him they needed to talk before she went over there.

"Hey," he said, stepping in front of her to block her view of the café. "Martin and I already told them this was highly inappropriate. Rich isn't too happy with them either. You don't have to talk to them."

"What else did you tell them?" she asked, putting her hand on her hip. "We haven't even talked about what I'm going to do."

"Nothing. I said that you needed time and they needed to respect that," he said. "My boss is pushing for a quick answer but he really knows that you need time. Even without Rich's signature on the documents, you have the text where he denies the child and waives his rights. So, them pushing you is at their own peril."

She tipped her head to the side, her expression had changed. She took his hand and drew him away from the café, up the block and around the corner.

"What does that mean?"

"Just that I'm not going to let them bully you. I think they thought you were some poor little accountant. They didn't realize who your folks are or who you were. Rich's mom loves the Candied Apple & Café by the way. She's mentioned it at least seven times this morning."

Cici shook her head. "I'd pretty much decided to get Rich's perspective on everything this morning, but I don't want to block them from knowing their grandchild. I wish they'd given the time I requested."

"You can have it. I will be happy to go over there and tell them to back off," he said.

"No. Thank you for the offer. But the baby is mine and I am the one who needs to do this."

Hoop wasn't sure what that meant but he knew that for the time being he had to give her the space she requested. "Do you want me to go with you?"

She squeezed his hand. "Yes. Just for moral support."

"You got it."

"Thanks, Hoop," she said.

"That's what I'm here for. I know it's not the right time to talk but I am always going to be here for you."

She hugged him. "I know. Thank you."

"You're welcome. Let's go take care of this situation so we can enjoy the rest of our day."

They made their way to the café. Rich was having a heated discussion with his parents. Hoop noticed that Cici hesitated. Finally, Rich looked up and when he did, he seemed surprised to notice they were holding hands.

"Hi, Rich," Cici said. "I'm surprised to see you here."

Rich rubbed the back of his neck. "Me too. Sorry for just showing up. I found out last night that my parents had been texting you from my phone. These are my parents, Richmond and Jill. Mom and Dad, this is Cici. Also, this is Martin Reynolds."

Martin and Richmond stood up and held their hands out to Cici.

"I'm sorry. We have been taken completely by surprise by this news and we are overjoyed" Richmond said. "But Rich ..."

"Dad. I meant it. Keep the criticism to a minimum or else," Rich said.

Hoop realized there was a lot of tension at the table and he didn't have to glance at Cici to know she was aware of it as well.

"Mr. and Mrs. Hallifax, I already know where Rich stands. We don't know each other at all. We were both feeling a little down that night and hooked up. That should have been it. I'm not sure what happened but now there is this baby. It never occurred to me that you ... well, even existed. Sorry, but I have been too busy dealing with what to do next."

"We understand that," Mr. Hallifax said.

"Thank you. I haven't had a chance to discuss this with my lawyer but I am open to you getting to know the child. I am extremely lucky to have three sets of grandparents and I know how valuable those relationships have been in my life. So, I'd love to talk to you more about this."

Mrs. Hallifax nodded. "That's all we really want. When Martin called us, we were taken by surprise and Richmond went into full on CEO mode determined to ..."

She trailed off but Cici just smiled ruefully at her. "Determined to get the child no matter how you had to do it."

"Yes. It wasn't fair to you," Rich's mom said.

"No, it wasn't," Cici agreed. "But I understand where you are coming from."

"Listen, I am still not ready to be a father," Rich said. "I am giving up my rights to the baby. My career is taking off and I have a fiancée and I want to focus on that."

"You have an obligation," Richmond said sternly.

"You can discuss that as a family," Cici said. "We can work out some sort of arrangement for you as grandparents. Rich and I know where we stand."

"I will work on something with Lilia at the office on Monday," Martin said. "We will make sure the arrangement suits all of you and be in touch next week."

Lucy tugged on her leash and Cici made her goodbyes, turning to lead the dog down the street to a grassy area. She was very aware of Martin making arrangements to meet with Rich's parents in his office next week.

Meeting with them wasn't as hard as she'd expected it to be. And seeing Rich again made her realize how little they had in common. He wasn't the kind of man she was attracted to normally and if it weren't for the baby growing inside of her, Rich would be one of the biggest regrets of her life.

But she had her bean.

"Mind if I walk back with you?" Hoop asked as he caught up with her.

"Nope," she said. "I was going to ask your advice before I went to meet with Rich this morning but I guess I didn't need it. His parents seem nice enough."

"They do. I think the strained relationship with Rich is really putting them in a difficult spot."

"It is," she agreed. "So why did you really stop when you saw Martin this morning?"

She didn't for one minute believe they had waved Hoop down. He wasn't the kind of man to avoid a situation.

"I didn't want Martin surprising you. I was pissed, if you want to know the truth. We had a great day yesterday and you needed the time to relax and figure out what to do," he said.

206

"My protector."

Hoop stopped and took her hand in his, their fingers linked together perfectly. She realized how much she wanted him by her side. Not because she needed a man or couldn't do it on her own, but because having him with her on this adventure would make life a little bit richer and much sweeter. "I want to be that and more."

"Do you?"

"Yes," he said. "Why do you think I keep chasing after you?"

"I guess you can't resist me," she said, being cheeky because the truth felt too important at this moment. She didn't want to admit how much she needed him.

"Are you joking?"

"A little," she said. "But only because I'm sort of scared and excited all at once. I've been falling for you a little bit more every day and I have always picked the worst men in the world to fall for."

"I'm not like them," Hoop said. "I'm certainly not like Rich."

"No. You aren't and I think I knew that from the first time we danced together at the Olympus," Cici said. "I think … I mean I know … that I love you. There, I've said it. And I want you in my life but you deserve someone who is all yours. Someone you can get to know before you have to share them with a child. And you deserve your own child," Cici said. "Not another …"

"Stop. I don't know what I deserve. My Pops always says the world doesn't owe any of us anything. What I *do* know is that I love you too, Cici. You have sent me into a tailspin from the moment we met and I haven't come out of it yet."

"Really?" she asked.

"Yes. I think that's why I pushed back the night at the club. Not a definite no, but more of a holy hell how am I going to keep up with this sexy, little dynamo. And I didn't. I let you go and immediately regretted it. You deserved a better man. And I am ready to be that man, if you'll have me."

He pulled her closer to him as Lucy circled around their feet, tangling the leash around their legs. "I want to spend the rest of my life with you, Cici. And I want to have this baby and many more. I think it's too soon to ask you to marry me. I want to wait so you can be sure of this. But you should know that is my intention."

She put her hands on either side of his face and leaned up to kiss him, trusting him to keep her safe as their lips met. The kiss was sweet and deep and an affirmation of everything that he had pledged to her.

"I want that too."

He lifted her off her feet and kissed her even more deeply. She knew that she'd found the love of her life and she knew they were going to have a wonderful life together.

Epilogue

Fourth of July two years later and Cici and Hoop were back in the Hamptons. Cici was pregnant with Hoop's baby and their almost two-year-old Holly was sleeping on Hoop's chest as he lay in a hammock in their backyard under the shade of a large tree. Cici put her hand on her stomach and just watched the father and daughter.

There was no doubt in her mind, nor would there ever be in Holly's, that Hoop loved her.

"Stop drooling over your man," Hayley said, coming into the kitchen followed quickly by Iona.

"You're just saying that because Garrett isn't in the backyard," Cici said.

"So true," Hayley said. "And I've been waiting until I had the two of you alone to tell you my news."

Iona draped an arm around Hayley's shoulder. "You're pregnant?"

"Yes. I'm not even mad you guessed. I ... you know we wanted to wait after we got married and we are going to tell everyone this weekend. Couldn't let you and Cici be the only moms in the group."

"We are happy to invite you into our Mom Club," Cici said.

"We definitely are," Iona added.

"Who would have thought that we'd end up here?" Cici said. "Our lives are so full."

Her friends agreed with her and then left to find their husbands. She drifted outside and Hoop looked up as she approached. He shifted to sit up, careful to keep Holly in his arms and not jostle.

"You look happy," she said.

"I am. I finally have the family I always wanted," he said.

"Me too."

Acknowledgements

I have to thank Charlotte Ledger my wonderful editor for her patience and support when I said I wanted to write a book where the heroine had slept with a guy, got pregnant and he wasn't the hero. Also, thanks to Eve and Nancy who spent endless hours on FaceTime with me as I wrote this book and needed a sounding block. As always, every book I write is made possible by the support of my loving husband Rob Elser and my two kiddos Courtney & Lucas.

Printed by RR Donnelley at Glasgow, UK